D1222585

THE TURNING

ALSO BY GLORIA WHELAN

THE TURNING

GLORIA WHELAN

Gloria Whelan
7/29/06

HARPERCOLLINS*PUBLISHERS*

The Turning

Copyright © 2006 by Gloria Whelan
www.harperchildrens.com

Library of Congress Cataloging-in-Publication Data
Whelan, Gloria.

The turning / Gloria Whelan.— 1st ed.

p.   cm.

Summary: In the months leading up to the August 1991
coup attempt that resulted in the collapse of communism in
the Soviet Union, a young dancer with the Kirov Ballet
struggles to decide whether to defect while on an upcoming
trip to Paris.

ISBN-10: 0-06-075593-8 (trade)

ISBN-13: 978-0-06-075593-5 (trade)

ISBN-10: 0-06-075594-6 (lib. bdg.)

ISBN-13: 978-0-06-075594-2 (lib. bdg.)

1. Soviet Union—History—Attempted coup, 1991—
Juvenile fiction. [1. Soviet Union—History—Attempted
coup, 1991—Fiction. 2. Kirov Ballet Company—Fiction.
3. Defectors—Fiction. 4. Ballet dancing—Fiction.
5. Conduct of life—Fiction. 6. Saint Petersburg (Russia)—
History—20th century—Fiction.] I. Title.
PZ7.W5718Tur 2006   2005008777
[Fic]—dc22   CIP
                                               AC

1 3 5 7 9 10 8 6 4 2
❖
First Edition

To Renée Cafiero
and all my copy editors at HarperCollins,
those strict mothers who keep me
from terrible danger

THE TURNING

ESCAPE

The moment my friend Vera Chikov heard our Leningrad ballet troupe would be going to Paris in August to perform, Vera began to plot her escape from the Soviet Union.

"Come with me, Tatiana," she begged. "Russia is dreary, like a picture painted all in gray and black. No excitement, nobody laughs, everyone is gloomy."

At first I could not take Vera seriously, but she talked about defecting day and night, exploring the possibilities as if she were an empress turning over the diamonds in her jewelry box. Instead of frightening her, the danger of defecting only made her more determined. I couldn't help but be impressed by Vera's courage.

After a while and just for the fun of it, I began to daydream about a life away from the Soviet Union. In the corner of our family apartment where I slept, I tacked up pictures of the river Seine and the Eiffel Tower and the Luxembourg Gardens, where you could sit by a little lake and read anything you wanted without worrying about someone reporting you to the KGB, the secret police. My favorite picture was of the Paris Opéra. I imagined myself dancing in that elegant building. Underneath the opera house was the grotto where the Phantom of the Opera was said to have lived. In the opera house museum you could see the ballet slippers of the great Russian dancer Vaslav Nijinsky and the crown Anna Pavlova, the most famous Russian ballerina of them all, wore when she danced *Swan Lake*.

I didn't want to leave my family, but the ballet meant everything to me. For as long as I could remember, I had sacrificed my life to endless hours of practice. Yet hard as I worked, I wondered if I would ever find in Russia the opportunity to further my career that I could find with the ballet of the Paris Opéra, or an even greater dream, the New York City Ballet in America. What at first began as an idle daydream began to be a possibility.

Vera told me of her plans: what she would take with her when she left Russia, and how, once she was in Paris, she would slip away and contact the authorities there, asking for asylum. It was hard not to be caught up in her excitement. We tried to guess what our chances would be of joining the Paris ballet. All these conversations were whispered. We knew what danger there would be in defecting. If we were caught, we would be thrown out of the ballet, perhaps arrested, certainly watched day and night. I was not sure I was willing to take the risk.

Vera shrugged off the danger. "The first thing I will do in Paris," Vera announced, "is go to the

Galeries Lafayette, the fancy department store, and buy lipstick that doesn't go on as if it were wax and a dozen pairs of those sexy French thong panties. Then I'm going to a restaurant and order a big goose liver and two kinds of soufflé for dessert."

I laughed at Vera's gluttony. "You'll get fat and won't fit into the panties," I told her. Vera's whole family was as hungry for things as Vera was. Unlike my family, her family had money, lots of it. The Chikovs' apartment was ten times bigger than ours. Vera had a bedroom all to herself. There was a room just for eating in and a living room where no one had to sleep. There was a television set where Vera and I could see the things that went on in the world, though most of what was going on in 1991 seemed to be bad news: war in the Middle East; in Afghanistan a thousand people dead in an earthquake. In Leningrad, where we lived, it wasn't much better. Night after night a TV show, *600 Seconds*, showed scenes of robberies and murders right in our own city.

Crowded into the Chikovs' kitchen were a stove with four burners and a refrigerator and even a microwave oven. I loved to put a cup of water in the little oven's belly and watch as the water boiled up. It was magic. Vera, who was one of the most generous people in the world, would give me a packet of American chocolate to put into the boiling water, and I would drink the heavenly cocoa.

The Chikovs were very rich, but no one was sure just why. They had a peephole in their apartment door so they could see who was knocking, and when I came to visit, I had to wait while they snapped open a dozen locks. Vera didn't walk to ballet rehearsals and performances but was taken and picked up in a car driven by a bodyguard. The car wasn't a cheap little Lada, or even a Volga, but a Mercedes from Germany. There were even rumors that the Chikovs' car was bulletproof.

Vera's father was once high up in the army, but his money did not come from that, for most of the soldiers in Russia hardly earned enough to feed their families. Mr. Chikov was no longer in uniform. He wore a navy-blue jacket with gold buttons and gray flannel trousers and carried a real leather briefcase. The rumor among the dancers was that Mr. Chikov was part of the newly rich who made their money in the black market buying and selling scarce goods. The newspaper was full of scandals. Millions of rubles' worth of caviar had been secretly shipped out of Russia labeled as herring! I wondered if it was caviar that Vera's father sold or something more dangerous.

For myself, I wouldn't go to Paris for fancy underwear. I told Vera, "After I sent money home, I'd buy toe shoes that don't have to be darned every five minutes." After our conversations about remaining in Paris, I began to see myself in Paris; at first it was only a harmless daydream, but bit by bit the daydream became more real. Vera had planted a seed, and what started as an impossible idea took root.

On this February day Leningrad was covered with

snow, and I thought how wonderful it would be to live in a country where you could practice in a heated rehearsal room. In our rehearsal room ice had formed on the insides of the windowpanes. Our breath when we spoke came out in little white puffs. When I stretched my arms out in an *arabesque*, it was nearly impossible to arrange my cold, stiff fingers into a graceful pose.

Our rehearsals were held in the Kirov Theater. It used to be the Mariinsky Theater, named after the wife of Tsar Alexander II, but after the Communist revolution tsars and their wives fell out of favor. The name was changed to honor Comrade Sergey Kirov, who was the head of the Communist party in Leningrad and who was assassinated in 1934. I knew all about that because my great-grandmother and great-grandfather, although they had nothing to do with killing Kirov, were exiled and sent off to Siberia in the arrests that followed Kirov's assassination. My great-grandfather died after becoming ill in one of Stalin's prison camps.

8

Though there was not enough money to heat the rehearsal rooms properly, the Kirov Theater itself, all blue and gold, was elegant with its magnificent bronze chandelier and painted ceiling. When I first performed at the Kirov, I wanted to get down on my knees and kiss the stage! I could hardly dance for the thought that this was the stage on which Pavlova and Nijinsky had danced. From the stage you looked out at a tiered half circle of a hundred boxes all decorated in gilt and velvet, where people with money or power sat. In the center of the theater was the box reserved for members of the government like Mikhail Gorbachev, who was both head of the Communist party and the president of the Soviet Union. Long, long ago the tsar and the empress of Russia had sat in that box. After the revolution Lenin had said ballet was useless. He wanted the theater closed down, but even Lenin could not keep Russians from their beloved ballet.

Our shabby rehearsal rooms were far away from all the grandeur of the theater. Madame Pleshakova, our ballet mistress, who oversaw our practice, marched into the room and called sharply to us. "Tanya, Vera, why aren't you at the barre practicing your *pliés*? Don't think for a minute you will be allowed to take the tour with us if you are lazy. Remember, not everyone will go. You must earn your way. With no discipline, all the talent in the world does not matter."

I loved Madame when she was fierce. She had once been a famous ballerina and had danced with the great Rudolf Nureyev before he had defected to America. Madame still had great elegance and grace. Her graying hair was pulled back into a tight chignon, and she always wore a long black skirt and a black sweater as if she were in constant mourning. There were wrinkles at the corners of her dark eyes, eyes that were hooded and could look sleepy until they opened wide and fixed on you so that you withered under their stab. Even the men in the ballet corps could be reduced to tears by her attacks. Still we loved her, for we understood she wanted us to be the best we could be, which was what we wanted too.

Our daily lesson had been called for eight in the morning, but by quarter to eight the corps was in place, some of us at the barre, some practicing in the center of the room. Vitaly, as usual, was leaping about, showing off his *jetés*. The heat from so many bodies began to warm the practice room. The skin of ice on the windows melted, and Aidan, our practice pianist, took off her gloves with the fingers cut out. I did my *pirouettes*, careful to keep my eyes focused on one spot in front of me, so that as I spun around I wouldn't get dizzy and my head would always snap back, giving the impression I was facing forward. Around and around I turned until I began to feel I had lost control of my body and it was spinning of its own accord. It was at that moment that I was always happiest, when my body took over from my mind.

All around me the other members of the corps were working as hard as I was. There had always been competition among us, but now, knowing that some of us would not make the tour, there was out-and-out rivalry and even jealousy. Usually you work in the corps de ballet at least three years before you graduate to small roles and finally to principal parts. I was sixteen, and as one of the youngest members of the corps, I had been teased and petted, but after I was given a principal part, I became a threat. Several times during the morning I had seen Marina watch me. If icy stares could kill, I would surely be dead. Marina and I were taking turns dancing the role of Juliet in *Romeo and Juliet*. She was incensed at having to share the part. I understood why she was so angry. She had been with the corps six years longer than I had, but I had overheard Madame say about me, "Tanya has such expressive arms, and for the part of Juliet one must have a *devochka*." At twenty-four, Marina was no longer a young girl.

Marina was also *arqué*, a fancy French word for bowlegged; most ballet terms come from the French language. *Arqué* is not as bad as it sounds. All ballet dancers are either bowlegged or knock-kneed. If you are bowlegged, you are strong but more rigid in your dancing. If you are *jarreté*, or knock-kneed, you are more graceful, with high, lovely insteps that unfortunately are sometimes weak. I was *jarreté*, which was better for Juliet. Fortunately my instep is as strong as leather.

Everyone in the troupe was a little in awe of Marina because her father was high up in the government. I always felt she was watching my every move and would report me to her father if I said something critical about the government or Russia's President Gorbachev.

By the time we broke for lunch, one of the blisters on my foot had opened, my ankle was wobbly, my leotard was damp with sweat, and I was starved. Watching my weight as usual, all I had allowed myself for breakfast was a glass of kefir. It was Vitaly's turn to buy the *pelmeny*, little dumplings filled with ground beef and cabbage or sometimes with cheese. Vitaly got them at the nearby *pirozhkovye*. The snack bar knew the little dumplings were for the corps de ballet and stuffed them generously. The proprietor believed we were all too thin and needed fattening, but we knew if we gained too much weight we would be thrown out of the troupe. Our stomachs had to be flat, and our chests, too, though for some of us that meant a lot of squeezing into tight bras.

Vitaly was like a great yellow cat with his blond hair, his green eyes, and his ability to stretch his limbs into graceful lines. He was a show-off, but so good-natured and so ready to laugh at himself, no one minded. He had struggled harder than any of us to be a dancer. His father had been one of the Soviet soldiers stationed in Hungary to keep that country under Soviet control. When Hungary, demanding its free-dom from the Soviet Union, sent the soldiers packing, the soldiers discovered there were no jobs and no housing for them back in Russia. Vitaly's father, whom Vitaly always referred to as the "Old Soldier," longed for the days when Stalin sent his armies everywhere. Vitaly confided in me that his father was angry about everything, but he was especially angry because Vitaly wanted to be a dancer. When Vitaly was accepted in ballet school, his father threw him out of the house, calling him a sissy. Only Vitaly's mother's pleading allowed him to return home. Now that Vitaly was doing well and could be seen performing on the stage, his father was almost reconciled to his son being a dancer. The Old Soldier was even boasting to all his friends that his son was sure to be traveling to Paris.

Vitaly was not so sure he would be going to Paris. His competition was Gregory. Gregory was not as good a dancer as Vitaly, but he was showy and had taken a dislike to Vitaly because Vitaly came from a poor family that had no tradition of culture. Gregory's grandmother had been a ballerina with the Kirov. "That makes me a member of the family," he said. He thought he was entitled to the best roles, but he refused to work for them as Vitaly did. Instead, he took every opportunity to make Vitaly look awkward. For the most part, Vitaly ignored Gregory, but I didn't underestimate Gregory's ambition.

Gregory was watching as Vitaly held up the latest issue of *Ballet* magazine and waved it in front of me. "Tanya," Vitaly said, "what will you give me to see your picture in the magazine?"

"Don't be foolish, Vitaly," I said, and punched him lightly in the arm.

"If I let you see it, will you let me practice my new way of doing lifts with you?"

"Toss me around all you like, but if I live to be a hundred I'll never find my picture in that magazine."

"Don't forget, you promised." Vitaly flipped open the magazine to an article on the ballet's performance of *Romeo and Juliet*. The picture had been taken on one of the evenings I had danced Juliet. My heart was a fluttering bird. When I lunged for the magazine,

Vitaly held it over his head. "Remember your promise."

"Yes, yes, but don't torment me, Vitaly."

Some of the other members of the corps, seeing the scuffling, joined us. Looking over Vitaly's shoulder, we read the article. Gregory, who was a friend of Marina's, scuttled over to her and whispered in her ear. Her expression froze and she stalked out of the room.

Vera said, "She'll never forgive you for your picture being in the magazine instead of hers."

I knew some of the members of the corps believed I had fallen into the role as a piece of luck. That was not true. I had been working toward it nearly all my life. As a special treat for my fifth birthday my great-aunt Marya, who loved everything beautiful, had taken me to see *Swan Lake* danced. How I had marveled at the elegance and grace of the dancers. I was sure they must live in a different world, a world where people could move about in new and wonderful ways.

I was so enchanted with the ballet that when the wicked magician tricked the prince, I cried out aloud to warn him, causing my aunt great embarrassment.

After seeing *Swan Lake*, I gave my parents no peace until they allowed me to try out for ballet school. For eleven years I lived and breathed dancing. I dreamed every night of being a prima ballerina assoluta. It did not discourage me that in two hundred years the Russian Imperial Theater had given the title to only two ballerinas. When I wasn't practicing, I was soaking my poor feet, binding up my wounded toes, massaging the knots and cramps in my legs, and mending my shoes, which cost a fortune.

The school was free, for the Soviet Union took great pride in its ballet; but practice clothes and ballet shoes were horribly expensive. Every penny my parents could spare went toward my dream. My mother, Svetlana, worked for only a pittance at the Hotel Europa as a chambermaid, and my father, Ivan, earned little more as a doctor. My grandfather Georgi and my grandmother Yelena pitched in from their small pensions to help support my dancing. Sometimes I felt guilty, knowing all the things the family went without, but when I said so, my grandmother Yelena told me, "Tanya, the dreams we have for you are worth all the rubles in the world to us." Now that I was thinking of defecting, I saw my family proudly reading about me as the star in the Paris ballet. If I became a famous ballerina in Paris or America, I could repay them.

"Vitaly," I pleaded, "lend me the magazine to take home for the night." I couldn't wait to show the family that their sacrifices were worth something.

"I'll make you a present of the magazine, Tanya, but stop eating so many *pelmeny* or I'll never be able to lift you." I threw my arms around him. "Don't smother me, Tanya." He pulled away and called to the pianist, Aidan, "Come and have some of the dumplings before Tanya eats them all."

Each day we made a point of inviting Aidan to share our lunch, guessing it might be the only decent meal she had that day. At first she had refused, but her hunger and our goodwill were too much for her and now she came each day willingly. Aidan's family were Russians who had been sent to Lithuania in the 1920s by the Soviets when they took it over. The Soviets wanted to put as many Russians there as possible. They wanted to colonize Lithuania with hundreds of thousands of Russians so that Lithuania would not try to free itself. A year ago, in 1990, Lithuania had declared its independence from the Soviet Union and was chasing the Russians home. What was happening in Lithuania was happening in all the Baltic countries. The Soviet Union had fought back. Gorbachev had sent Soviet tanks into Lithuania. But the desire for independence was growing in all the republics of the Soviet Union, such as the Ukraine and Georgia. In far-away Chechnya Russian soldiers had been called in to put down an uprising. The people in those republics were tired of being colonized by Russians and angry that the Russians had taken all the best bits of their land. They wanted freedom and democracy, something the Soviet Union had never allowed them.

Once the Russians were expelled back to Russia, like the returning Soviet soldiers, there was no housing for them and no jobs. In Lithuania Aidan had been a well-known pianist. Her husband had been a leader in the Communist party. Here in Russia, at forty years old, Aidan could not find concert work and earned only a few rubles for playing for our practice sessions. She was bitter toward the Lithuanians. "I never asked to go to their miserable country," she said. "It was my grandparents who were sent by the Soviet government. Now the government will do nothing for us." But she was even more bitter toward Gorbachev. "If he were a proper Communist, he would have seen that the Russians remained in Lithuania. He would have sent more soldiers. What we need is a stronger Communist party."

I was sorry for Aidan, but I was all for the Lithuanians. After years of being trampled on by the

Soviet Union, the Lithuanians wanted to be free of Russians. Only a week ago Russian tanks had lumbered into Vilnius, the capital of Lithuania. Fourteen Lithuanians fighting for their freedom from Russia had been killed and many more crushed under the tanks. Vera and I had seen pictures on *The Fifth Wheel*, the Leningrad TV show, of Russian soldiers crushing the Lithuanians. I didn't understand how Aidan could see such pictures and still think the Russians should rule Lithuania.

"Aidan, there are more dumplings than we can eat," I said. "Here is a bit of greased paper. Wrap them up and take them home for your husband." Aidan's husband had no job. Some days Aidan came to practice with red eyes and sometimes—it broke our hearts to see it—with bruises. We guessed that her husband in his misery got hold of vodka, which brought out a cruel streak.

The heat from our bodies and the dumplings in my belly made me sleepy, but one word from Madame and

I was wide-awake, and at my *chassés*, my *battements*, my *pirouettes*. Soon I was nothing but a streak of energy existing only for movement's sake. From the corner of my eye I saw Marina watching me. If I did fifty *battements*, she did sixty. If I did a dozen *pirouettes*, she did two dozen. Her jealousy set her on fire. Finally Madame called, "Marina, it is not how many, but how well. Don't just do, think of what you are doing." After that, even more of Marina's dark looks were sent my way.

CHAPTER 2

POLITICS

When rehearsal ended, it was four in the afternoon and already quite dark. In winter, daylight in Leningrad was as rare as darkness was in the summer. I threw on my jacket, pulled a knit cap over my hair, and ran out the door. If I hurried, I just had time to get to Vasilievsky Island and the Academy of Arts, where Sasha's classes would be ending. I couldn't wait to show him the magazine. The streetlights were on, and in their glow the fine snow that was sifting down turned golden. When I started across the bridge, the wind all but picked me up and nearly blew me down onto the icy Neva River. I hung on to the railing, feeling the cold of the iron through my mittens. The backs of the ancient stone sphinxes that crouched on either side of the academy were covered in snow, a strange sight on statues that had come from the deserts of Egypt. Students poured out of the Arts Academy, brushing past me, eager to get home to warmth and dinner. At last I saw Sasha.

He was eighteen, two years older than I was. His face was long and thin, with high cheekbones and dark eyes that turned down at the corners. When he thought to wash his hair, it was very nice and curled at his shoulders. He was like a birch sapling, thin as a whip and birch-bark white because he never got out of doors. He was either in class at the academy or in the corner of his grandmother's room, working on his paintings or on the icons he sold to tourists. Icons are paintings of sacred people—saints and angels and the holy family. The old icons are said to have special powers of protection and healing and have been handed down from generation to generation.

Sadly, many of the ancient icons were destroyed when the Communists ordered the churches closed and emptied.

Sasha's icons were popular, for it was illegal to sell the old icons and Sasha had learned what kind of paint and gilt to use to give his copies an ancient look. Money from the sale of the icons helped to keep his grandmother in medicine. Sasha's parents had died when he was a baby, and his grandmother had raised him. He never talked of his parents. Many families in the Soviet Union had been broken up by arrests and disappearances, my own family among them. It was best not to ask too many questions. One of the most imposing buildings in the city of Leningrad was at 4 Liteyny Prospekt, the home of the KGB, the secret police. Thousands and thousands had entered those doors and disappeared, the lucky ones to exile in Siberia.

The joke was "What is the tallest building in Leningrad?"

"The KGB building. You can see Siberia from its basement."

I waved the magazine in front of Sasha, and we huddled together, sheltering the magazine from the snow, while Sasha read the article. "Ah, Tanya," he said, "now you will be so conceited you won't want to look at a poor peasant like me."

I poked him in the ribs. "Don't tease me, Sasha. I'm afraid the article means trouble for me. Marina looked daggers at me today."

"That old lady. You can dance circles around her."

Sasha saw the ballet whenever he had a few extra rubles. Many of his paintings were of dancers. I had met him when he came to our rehearsal room and sweet-talked Madame into letting him draw the dancers while they practiced. She was indignant and tried to throw him out, but while she was shouting at him he drew her and then showed her the drawing with her mouth open and her fist raised. At first she was furious, then she began to laugh. "Ah, you are a clever fellow. Very well. You may stay for an hour, but no longer, and you are not to talk to the dancers. Not one word. If you disturb their work, you are out on your bottom."

He had not said a word but he had managed to pass me a note that said "I'm going to spend my life drawing you."

Before he left Madame demanded to see his work. "Well, you are a perceptive fellow. You have a talent for capturing the grace of dancers. It almost reminds me of Degas's sketches, but don't let that go to your head. You are a long way from the master."

After that she allowed him to return, and each week, on his day off from the academy, he sat quietly in the corner sketching us. One afternoon he walked home with me. After that we began to see each other, spending hours in the *pyshechnayas*, the doughnut shops, over a cup of coffee. I told myself we were just good friends, but the truth was Sasha was becoming more and more important to me. When something happened, it didn't seem real until I told Sasha about it. It was a terrible effort to keep secret from Sasha the idea that I might defect, but Vera had sworn me to secrecy. I wanted to share everything with Sasha. When I saw the article in the magazine, I thought at once of him.

"I'll treat you to the metro," I said, and the two of us ducked into the entrance of the underground station to escape the snow and raw wind. At the bottom of the stairway, the station was like a grand ballroom with marble walls and crystal chandeliers, but no one behaved like they were in a ballroom. Everyone pushed and shoved for a place in one of the cars. Sasha hung on to me, taking the excuse of the crowding to hug me close, causing one woman to frown and another to smile. Sasha kissed the top of my head, winking impertinently at the first woman and grinning at the second.

It was only a short distance to our stop, but the line ran beneath the frozen Neva River. It was always amazing to me to have the river over my head, as if I were a mermaid in some magic kingdom under the sea. We emerged from the metro stairway onto the Nevsky Prospekt. The headlights of the cars illuminated the curtain of falling snow, and along the Prospekt the streetlamps washed the buildings with light. With Sasha clasping my arm, everything seemed bright and cheerful. I glanced up at Sasha to see if he was as happy as I, and was taken aback to see a worried expression on his face.

"Sasha, what is it?" I asked.

"It's my grandmother, Tanya. The only place I can find the medicine she needs is on the black market, and the cost there is more than we can afford. I am painting on both sides of my canvases to save money."

"Sasha, what can you do?"

His face became tighter, more closed in. "Never mind. I'll find a way. Go home and show your family how famous you are." He gave me a hug and was soon lost in the crowds.

I tucked the magazine inside my coat to keep it dry. For the thousandth time I thought of the escape Vera and I were planning. It would be hard to leave Sasha. Where would I find someone who understood me so well, someone who knew what I was thinking before I knew it myself? Then I thought of Sasha's struggles to take care of his grandmother. What kind of life could Sasha and I have together? If I escaped, I would leave behind me all the sad stories, all the miseries of people like Sasha's grandmother and Aidan and her husband and Vitaly. My grandfather Georgi kept saying that a new day would come for Russia, but how could I believe him? If I wanted happiness, I would have to risk the danger of finding it in another country. I would have to dance my way to it.

By the time I reached our apartment building on the Prospekt, the snow was a sloppy porridge. The building, which stood across from Kazan Cathedral, was once known as the Zhukovsky mansion. It had started out life as the home of an aristocrat, and not just any aristocrat. My grandfather says it once belonged to my great-grandmother Katya's family. When the revolution came, the family fled for their lives. Grandfather remembers how as a little boy his mother would take him and his sister, my great-aunt Marya, to see the mansion. His mother had told them stories of how her own mother had been a lady-in-waiting to Empress Alexandra. She had even shown him pictures of the four daughters of the empress and the tsar, pictures that had come from a locket given to her by the empress herself. When two small rooms in the mansion became available, Grandfather had pleaded with the family to move there. Grandfather said, "How my mother would have rejoiced to see us living in even one of the rooms in which she grew up."

The apartment stairway had an elegant sweep to it, but it smelled of cabbage and bathrooms. This evening, and not for the first time, I had to stumble over a man sleeping off too much vodka. The apartment itself, which looked out onto the Prospekt, was shabby and moldering, but you could still see bits and pieces of its past glory, like a woman whose shabby dress is trimmed with a bit of real lace. The floors of our small sitting room, where my grandparents slept, were of inlaid wood, and there was a ring of faded flowers painted around the wall. Besides the sitting room there was a bit of a kitchen and a tiny bedroom for my parents. I slept in what must once have been a closet. Sometimes the gowns and furs that had hung there long ago crept into my sleep, and I dreamed I was dressed in satin and jewels, whirling around the ballroom of a palace.

Down the hall from our apartment was a bathroom we shared with several families. If you were not up at the crack of dawn, the hot water was gone. Still we were lucky. Aidan and her husband had to live in a communal shelter with not a thing to call their own.

In our apartment we lacked for room, but we never lacked for liveliness. There were cries of delight and much excitement over the article in the magazine, which was passed from hand to hand. Grandmother Yelena, who was the most emotional one in the family, had tears in her eyes. Grandmother worked in the Leningrad library, but her life was writing poetry. For many years she had not been allowed to publish her work. The Soviet Union had stilled the voices of all its great poets. Anna Akhmatova had been silenced and Osip Mandelstam was sent off to a prison camp to die. Grandmother says, "It brings tears to my eyes when I look at the shelves in the library and imagine all the books that aren't there. Somewhere there must be a ghostly library with the books of all those silenced writers." Tonight her tears were happy tears. She kissed me on both cheeks and hugged me to her.

"How proud your great-grandmother would be of you," Grandfather said. "When she was a young girl, she saw all the great ballerinas dance. She sat in the royal box with the tsar and the empress and their daughters. In those days the ballerinas had grand dukes falling at their feet, sending them armfuls of roses and precious jewels."

I said, "I would gladly settle for a big cabbage or a fat chicken."

"I have a better reward than that for my famous daughter," Mama said. She produced a package from the Hotel Europa, where she worked as a chambermaid. When she cleaned the rooms, she emptied the wastebaskets. The Americans and the Japanese had the best wastebaskets. Their baskets were full of treasure. There might be a pair of pantyhose with only a small run, a broken lipstick, or a can of hair spray that wasn't quite empty. There were American magazines and even books. Mama once found a pair of jeans with the knees worn out that Grandmother spoiled by patching when they would have been perfect with the holes.

There were some things Mama was forbidden to take. The little half-empty bottles of lotion and shampoo and the used bars of soap left behind by the tourists belonged to the head housekeeper, who sold them. If Mama took them, she would lose her job. She was not supposed to take toilet paper and Kleenex either, but every night she brought home a few sheets of each.

Mama opened her package and, as if she were taking a rabbit out of a hat, proudly produced a pair of women's shoes. The shoes were black patent leather. One of the heels was missing. Many of our streets are still made of cobblestones, so that was not the first pair of tourist shoes to be ruined. Peter the Great built St. Petersburg on swampy land where there were no stones, but when the city rose from that swamp, nearly three hundred years ago, Peter gave the order that every visitor to the city must bring three stones with him. People who wished to live in the city had to bring a hundred stones. From those stones Peter made our streets, and many of the stones are still there.

"The shoes can easily be repaired, and they are your size, Tanya. The soles of your own shoes have holes." Mama was so pleased with her gift. I tried to look grateful, but the truth was that they were old ladies' shoes, and I knew I would just stick them under my bed and wear my worn ones.

Father had been silent, as he always was when Mama brought things home. He hated to have her rummaging through wastebaskets. "Have you no pride, Svetlana?" he would say.

"Ivan," Mama would tell him, "if all you had to dress yourself with was pride, you couldn't appear in public."

On this day Papa said nothing, for he had other things on his mind. Papa—who practiced medicine at the Erisman Hospital, where my great-grandmother Katya had once been a nurse—worried day and night about the state of health in the Soviet Union. The week before, he had submitted an article to the medical society. He had warned that the death rate was spiraling. The twin curses of tuberculosis and AIDS were killing thousands. He hoped the article would rouse the government into doing something. Now, from the expression on his face, we could see his article had been returned. "What is the point?" he asked. "The government doesn't want to admit the truth. Our nurses must use dirty syringes because there is no money for new ones. The blood supply is contaminated. Our patients are sicker when they leave the hospital than when they enter."

Mama, whose answer to everything was food, began ladling out the soup. The tiny apartment was filled with the wonderful aroma of borscht. There were pieces of meat in the soup along with the cabbage and beets. There was even a spoonful of sour cream to go on top of each serving.

"How can you complain, Ivan?" Grandfather said. "Here we are all together filling our bellies. None of us is in a prison camp, and our own Tanya is growing into a fine ballerina. You don't know how lucky you are. You don't know what real suffering is. In the Great Patriotic War we ate pine bark and glue."

"Georgi," Grandmother said, "no one wants to hear about how bad things were in the old days."

"Well, then," Grandfather said, "let them think about what is going on now. We are just a month away from the election, and who is paying attention?"

I knew that we would not get through a meal without talk of politics. In our family everyone had an opinion and we kicked our opinions back and forth as if the kitchen table were a soccer field. It was politics for breakfast, lunch, and dinner. If politics were food, we would all have been fat as pigs. For generations our family had risked their lives to argue politics. My great-grandparents had been exiled to Siberia for speaking out. My grandparents had once been sent away as well. Now, in one month, there was to be an election, and everyone in the family had an opinion. Mikhail Gorbachev and Boris Yeltsin were running for different positions, but really they were running against each other for control of the Soviet Union. Gorbachev wanted to take baby steps in the direction of a democratic government; Yeltsin wanted to plunge right in.

Grandmother Yelena slapped her hand on the table. "I am paying attention. I'm voting for Gorbachev. He has given us perestroika, a new start, new thinking. He has relaxed censorship. Finally writers are seeing their work in print." Only the month before, Grandmother had had a poem published in the magazine *Literatura*.

Grandfather Georgi's face became red. "Perestroika! Where is it? What have we had from your Gorbachev? Five miserable years of broken promises. Even if you have the money, anything you buy is shoddy and useless. The government is full of bribery and thieves, and Gorbachev is afraid to do anything about it. The coal miners are striking for a living wage and our factories are shutting down for lack of coal. There are people starving and our great leader Gorbachev wants to double prices on food. And where is your Gorbachev now when there is work to be done? He is off in the Crimea, like an imperial tsar, basking in the sun in his twenty-million-ruble palace, while half the population starves and the army and the KGB plot against him."

"No one says things are perfect," Mama said, trying to calm things down by being on both sides at once. "but maybe the devil you know is better than the devil you don't know. Of course, Yeltsin has some good ideas."

"We must do something now," Grandfather said. "Things could not get worse than they have under Gorbachev. I mean to give Yeltsin a chance." For months Grandfather had been working on Yeltsin's election campaign in Leningrad.

"Just be careful, Georgi," Papa warned Grandfather. "Gorbachev is determined to silence Yeltsin. If you stick your neck out for Yeltsin, you may find a noose around it."

"Being careful is not in Georgi's nature." Grandmother sighed. "He has been fighting for freedom in this country as long as I have known him."

Papa said, "Anyhow, what good is an election when there is only one party, the Communist party, to vote for?"

"We mean to change that," Grandfather said. "People are resigning the party by the thousands. Unfortunately that only makes the party leaders more desperate. I'm afraid they are willing to do anything to hold on to their power."

All the discussion seemed foolish. What did it have to do with me? I had heard these arguments a thousand times. Nothing would change in Russia. Russia would never be a democracy. In Russia there seemed to be no future; in the outside world, anything seemed possible. Escape was the answer. If I decided to go with Vera, I would never have to listen again to the same old arguments.

I busied myself sewing ribbons on my ballet shoes. The shoes were terribly expensive, and you were lucky if you could get through a performance with only one pair worn out. I wore out nearly two hundred pairs a year, and each new pair had to be broken in before it could be worn. First, the sole had to be grated on Mama's potato grater so that I didn't slip. The box of the toe, the part that supports you when you are en pointe, had to be mercilessly hammered so that the box seemed a part of your foot. Finally, because I had the misfortune to have a second toe longer than the first toe, I had to stuff cotton in the shoe so all the toes were equal.

While the arguments continued, the door to the apartment opened, and there was Aunt Marya stamping her boots to get rid of the snow. She is really my great-aunt, but we are so close that I call her aunt. She has had great tragedy in her life. The man she was in love with, a soldier, Andrei, was killed in the last days of the Great Patriotic War. She never married but devoted her life to the Hermitage, Leningrad's great art museum.

It was difficult to find stylish clothes in the Soviet Union, but Aunt Marya was always stylish. It was as if the ravishing pictures she lived with all day in the museum lent her some of their elegance. She was wearing a wool cloak embroidered with flowers and a long matching skirt. Over this was thrown a wool shawl in a brilliant blue.

I longed to tell Aunt Marya that I was thinking of running away from the Soviet Union. I was sure she would be sympathetic, for she had once told me, "Tanya, many years ago I was invited to go to Paris when some of the paintings from the Hermitage were being displayed there. What a city! The boulevards, the Seine, the fashionable women, and Tanya, there are restaurants where you can order whatever you like. How I longed to stay, to escape all this dreariness. I could not. I couldn't leave all my lovely pictures in the Hermitage. It was during the days of Stalin. To get money for a bigger army, Stalin was selling some of our finest paintings to a rich man who had a museum in America. Though I knew I could do little about it, still, I had to be in Russia standing guard over the pictures. But Tanya, I have never forgotten Paris."

After she took off her boots, Aunt Marya kissed everyone and exclaimed over the article in the magazine. "I can tell from this article that the editor of the magazine has his eye on you, Tanya. You are sure to be picked to go on the tour to Paris, and how I envy you. You must visit all my favorite places for me."

Mama gave Aunt Marya a cup of hot tea and some bread and jam. "You are just in time to take sides," Mama said. "We are shouting at one another as to who is to lead the Soviet Union, Gorbachev or Yeltsin."

"We will be very lucky if that is our choice," Aunt Marya said.

"What do you mean, Marya?" Mama asked.

We all listened, for as second in command of the Hermitage, Aunt Marya overheard political gossip while showing groups of important politicians around the museum or attending receptions at which members of the government were present. The officials spoke more freely than they might have if they could have seen through Aunt Marya's charm to her sharp mind.

"We had a little contingent from the politburo yesterday," she said. "They came to see if they had received their money's worth for the fortune it had cost to clean the Leonardo da Vinci. I trailed along, smiling and smiling at them as they talked away. There seems to be a feeling that both Gorbachev and Yeltsin are embracing too much freedom to suit the old-line Communists. I believe they would like to get rid of both men. If the country is not careful, we will have another Stalin on our hands."

Grandfather's face was very red. "I hear the same thing. Nothing could be worse, but how could they fix the election? I don't see that it is possible."

Aunt Marya shrugged. "Georgi, you above all should know that in this country everything is possible."

After Aunt Marya left, I slipped away to my little

closet and emptied out my purse to see how many rubles I had. As soon as I had enough, I was going to buy a CD of French love songs sung by Jean Sablon and Charles Trenet. Their voices were so sexy. My aunt Marya had a CD player she let me use. I forgot all about politics and what might or might not happen to my country. What could that have to do with me? Instead, I imagined myself strolling along the Seine on a spring day with a debonair Frenchman. When a little voice inside me said, "What about Sasha?" I silenced it.

CHAPTER 3

SASHA

The next afternoon, on my way to the children's shelter where I volunteered as a ballet teacher, I stopped by to see Sasha. Home for Sasha and his grandmother was a walk-up apartment on a side street where even fifty years later you could still see bullet holes from the war. Sasha's grandmother, Nadya Petrovna, was sitting up in bed. She was like a bird with tiny sharp features and hair like feathers sticking up around her small head. Even her voice had a chirping sound. "Sasha, love, here is Tanya to see us. Just what I needed to cheer me. Come, sit on the bed, Tanya, and tell me about your dear family. Sasha, put on the kettle and give Tanya some of those American cookies you brought me." She shook her head. "My Sasha spoils me. Every day he brings me a present."

His generosity was one of the reasons I cared so much for Sasha. He never spent money on himself; any money that did not go for his art supplies went for his grandmother. Besides her medicines, he bought little treats to make her happy. I settled down beside Nadya Petrovna, and she grasped my hand in her hot, thin fingers. Her wasted body was wrapped in a brightly colored silk kimono. Sasha had traded one of his paintings for it. Nadya Petrovna looked like a creature from a fable, a fairy godmother or a kindly witch. The apartment was only one small room with a portion curtained off for Sasha, but it was magical. The tables and dresser tops were covered with bright scarves; even the lamps were draped with scarves, so the room was faintly lit in different colors. On the walls were Sasha's ballet sketches and paintings.

Along with Sasha's work, Nadya Petrovna had

several icons on the wall, all but one of them of little value except to her. Nadya Petrovna's icon of St. Vladimir had a place of honor. St. Vladimir lived more than a thousand years ago. He started out very badly, what with killing Christians right and left and having lots of wives and eight hundred girlfriends. Later in his life he repented, became a Christian, and said goodbye to the eight hundred girlfriends. A candle burned in front of the icon, which was old and very valuable. Nadya Petrovna once told me the ancient icon had come to her family in a mysterious way that was never spoken of aloud, but that had something to do with the Empress Alexandra herself. "We clung to it through revolution and war," she said.

The icons Sasha was working on were scattered on a table. He had once explained to me how he mixed his tempera paints in order to copy the soft blues, reds, and golds of the old icons. "Sasha, you are so clever," I said. "These look like they are hundreds of years old. I could never tell them from the real thing." Sasha merely shrugged. For all of his cleverness I knew he resented painting the icons and longed to have more time to spend on his own original work.

While Sasha put on the kettle, I turned to Nadya Petrovna. "Tell me how you are feeling," I said.

Though she was nothing more than skin and bones, and looked as if she would disappear in a puff of smoke at any moment, she answered, "Very well, my dear. My Sasha is a miracle worker. Somehow he finds me medicine." Papa often complained about a lack of medicine for his patients, and I knew Sasha had to buy the medicine on the black market and pay dearly for it.

Sasha came in bearing a tray with glasses of tea and a plate of dainty cookies. I longed to sample one, but Sasha did not take one and frowned at me, so I excused myself with "I am still full from lunch." I knew he wanted the treats for his grandmother.

I was startled to hear a chirping noise and thought for a moment it came from Nadya Petrovna. She was laughing at my surprise. "Sasha, take the scarf from the cage. Let Tanya see the little companion you have given me to cheer me up."

Sasha, looking embarrassed, pulled away one of the scarves, revealing a birdcage. Inside the cage a little finch hopped about, excited at the light.

"That's Kuzma. My little darling takes a nap when I do," Nadya Petrovna said. "When Sasha is gone, he keeps me company. We sing to each other." At this she began a chirping, peeping noise and the bird answered. "There, you see, we speak the same language." The difference between them was that the bird sang freely and Sasha's grandmother was soon out of breath.

I saw that Nadya Petrovna's face was paler than it had been when I first arrived and her eyelids drooped. Hastily I excused myself, promising to return. Sasha took up the glasses and disappeared into the kitchen.

"Come again soon," she whispered. "I like to have lively young people about." She held on to my hand.

Suddenly all her cheerfulness was gone. It was like seeing a bird dropping from the heavens to the ground. With a quick glance toward the kitchen, she whispered, "Promise me if anything happens to me, you will watch over Sasha."

I was going to reassure her that nothing would happen to her but I saw from her eyes that she did not want easy comforting. I held more tightly to her hand and nodded, hating myself for my deception, for I might be far away in Paris.

Sasha followed me into the hallway. I knew from his closed, sulky face that he did not want me to see how much he cared for his grandmother. I held his face in my hands and kissed him. "Sasha," I said, "Nadya Petrovna will be fine. With all your good care, how could she not be?"

As I left, I heard his grandmother say in a small breathless voice, "Sasha, dear, put the scarf over the cage. Kuzma and I will have a little rest."

I tried to put Sasha's troubles out of my mind as I

hurried along to the children's shelter, cutting through the Summer Garden where the rows of statues were covered with gray wooden boxes to protect them from the snow. Inside the boxes were Roman emperors and voluptuous women all waiting for the spring to set them free. It was like Russia itself, waiting for some miracle to turn it from a gray, drab country into the great land it had once been. Grandfather Georgi was an optimist, insisting that the people of Russia had survived revolutions and terror, starvation and war, so that one day they might be free. I could not be as optimistic as Grandfather, for the dream of Russia's freedom kept slipping away.

A few years ago some archaeologists, digging in the Summer Garden just where I was walking, found unexploded artillery shells from the Great Patriotic War. Fearing that the bombs might go off before they could be safely dug up and detonated, people from all over the city brought their old clothes and blankets to protect the elegant statues. I remembered Grandmother setting off for the garden with our only tablecloth. It was like that with Russia. It seemed as if there was always some emergency requiring its people to make sacrifices.

On the Prospekt people walked against the wind, their heads down, brushing past one another without a look. On Ostrovsky Square snow was wrapped about the statue of Catherine the Great like an ermine mantle. I turned into the ugly warehouselike building that housed the shelter. Most of the children were runaways, many of them children who had been abandoned and abused. There was a name for such children, *besprizorniki*, neglected ones. The name had first been used seventy-five years ago for the orphans of the revolution. After all the years of communism we still had to have shelters for *besprizorniki*. I admired Grandfather for working so hard for change, but it seemed it would never come.

Uncle Fyodor was in charge of the shelter and had talked me into giving ballet lessons to some of the children. Uncle Fyodor was not really my uncle. During the Siege of Leningrad Aunt Marya had found him abandoned, his parents dead of starvation, a *besprizornik* himself. She had adopted him. He had never forgotten her kindness and had given his life to the abandoned children of Leningrad.

He was a heavy man with a healthy appetite and a round belly to match. He had large features and a massive shiny bald head. Everything about Uncle Fyodor was big: his gestures, his round eyes, his wide smile, and his heart. It was hard to imagine the shy, skinny child Aunt Marya talked of rescuing.

I was greeted with a hug and nearly disappeared into Uncle Fyodor's big arms and chest. "Tanya, the children have been counting the hours until your arrival. They live for your visits. Let me take your coat and get rid of your wet boots."

I had been working with my class for over a year. It was small, only four children ten to twelve years old: Anatoli, Galina, Yulia, and Natalia. Anatoli had no discipline but jumped about as he pleased, thinking ballet was a kind of gymnastic exercise. Galina and Yulia were dear girls who were in love with the idea of becoming ballerinas, but who would be just as happy to be rock singers or movie stars. They only wanted a glamorous life and had no idea of the years of work it takes to learn ballet. It was Natalia who gave me hope. She was like me. If she had to give up dancing, I believed she would die.

When I first saw her, she had a bruise on her pinched face and a patch of her hair was missing. Even with her injuries she had a delicate beauty. She had come to the shelter because her father in one of his drunken rages had beaten her and her mother. The mother had stayed, but Natalia had run away.

She refused to say where she came from or what the rest of her name was. She insisted that she had run away only to be a ballerina. When she told Uncle Fyodor her story, he contacted me and the classes began. "There is very little for them here," he had said. "They need some occupation." While the other three children forgot about their dancing the minute the class was over, Uncle Fyodor said, Natalia practiced day and night.

For once Natalia's somber, pale face was flushed and excited. "Tanya," she said, "I have done a hundred and twenty *sur les pointes* on my new shoes. Soon I will have to darn them as you do." I had coaxed the members of the ballet troupe to save their worn toe slippers for me, and the last time I had come, I had brought four pairs.

I had to smile at how quickly she picked up the French words that are so much a part of the world of ballet. "Natalia, the minute you have new shoes, you want to wear them out!"

"But you are always complaining about darning your shoes."

"Yes, yes, but give yourself a little time. Now everyone at the barre." Uncle Fyodor had put a practice barre up against the wall of the little room that served as a cafeteria for the shelter at mealtimes. The shoes seemed to have enchanted the four children, and they worked earnestly at their exercises. To reward them, I told them the story of the famous red dancing slippers and how the little girl who wished for them got them and then couldn't stop dancing. The story gave me an idea. I would make up my version of a ballet about the shoes, and Natalia would dance the part of the girl. I had wanted to show her off to Madame Pleshakova, hoping that Madame would take her into the ballet school next year. If it was to happen, it must be soon, for Natalia was already old to begin her training.

I assigned parts and calmed Anatoli, who was rejoicing in the grisly part of the woodman who chops off the girl's feet. It was the first time the class had danced a story. In the beginning everyone was interested, but when Galina, Anatoli, and Yulia saw that each movement would have to be practiced over and over, they soon lost interest, just going through the motions. In Natalia the story ignited a fire. She practiced each step until she could dance it effortlessly. She *was* the girl who was dancing in enchanted slippers. Although the only training she had was the little I had given her, she was like a force of nature, like a tornado or a typhoon. There were mistakes and awkwardness, and her steps were simple ones, but with a deep sigh I wondered if with all my skill and practice I would ever have Natalia's fire.

GUILTY BY ASSOCIATION

The February snows melted into late-March fogs and into mists that rose from the rivers and canals and turned the city into an illusion of a city. Leningrad became St. Petersburg again, the city that Peter the Great was said to have built in the sky and then, when he had found just the right place, let down to earth.

Everything in my life was as up in the air as Peter's city. We had yet to learn who would be in the tour and who would be left behind. A great deal depended upon the ballets that would be danced. If we did the classical ballets such as *Sleeping Beauty* and *Swan Lake*, it might be one group of dancers. It might be another group of dancers if we did the more experimental ballets, like the new version of *The Rite of Spring* that we were premiering on this evening.

The Rite of Spring, with its discord and primitive rhythms, was demanding. The brilliant colors of the setting made an almost garish background. The choreographer had captured the wild frenzy of the music, so by the end of the evening's performance Vitaly had pulled a hamstring and Vera had twisted her knee. We were all exhausted and dreaded hearing the verdict of our director, who marched onto the stage the moment the curtain came down. If Madame was strict, Maxim Nikolayevich was a tyrant. The very sight of him made us cringe, yet any one of us would have given our life for him, for he was a genius. Now he began to shout, "You must all have been under the illusion that you were movie stars tonight. What smiles, what grimaces, what raised eyebrows and turned-up mouths. How often do I have to tell you—you do your acting with your arms and your feet. The emotion is in the music and in the dancing. *Please*, there is no need to make faces!"

That evening I kept Vera company in the Chikovs' apartment while she rubbed her poor knee with liniment. We drank the delicious cocoa and watched TV with her mother and father. I had heard from Grandfather that there were to be demonstrations all over the Soviet Union in support of Yeltsin. In the elections earlier in the month, Yeltsin had added to the ballot a question asking voters if they wanted to be able to vote directly for the president of Russia. Overwhelmingly they voted yes. For the first time the people of Russia would be able to elect their own president, and of course that would be Yeltsin. The demonstrations were meant to send a signal to Gorbachev that he was too slow in making the reforms he had promised. If he didn't move faster toward democracy, Yeltsin was now in a position to pressure him. An angry Gorbachev immediately outlawed the demonstrations. We watched as a commentator on the official government TV station denounced the demonstration leaders as hooligans. But I knew my grandfather, who planned to lead Leningrad's demonstration the next day, legal or illegal, was no hooligan.

Vera's father was furious with Yeltsin. "He is poking his nose into things that don't concern him," he said. "Let Yeltsin beware, or the army and the KGB will knock some sense into his thick head." I suspected that Yeltsin's reform of black market activities might be a threat to Vera's father's business, but I was drinking his cocoa and so I said nothing.

Vera said, "What do those old men have to do with me?" She took my hand. "Come away and let's talk of something more cheerful." She gave me a wink.

We sat in her bedroom and whispered about plans for defecting. "What if the Paris ballet doesn't take us?" I asked.

"Listen, Tanya," Vera promised, "you will have no trouble at all finding an important place with the Paris ballet. They would be thrilled to have you. I will be lucky to get a place in the company, but I don't care. I only want to leave this sinking boat that is Russia."

"I don't know," I said. "Sometimes I think it would be disloyal to leave."

"How could one person like yourself make any difference? Be realistic. Think what it would be like to walk into stores with the latest fashions instead of dresses that look like bags."

It wasn't for fashion that I would leave Russia. "If I go, Vera, it will be because I want a chance to be the best dancer I can be." I was still worried about the risk we would take. "What if someone discovers what we are doing? What if we are arrested?"

"My papa says you wouldn't believe what people get away with, and he should know. I've talked with someone who knew Nureyev. She told me how when he defected, everyone went out of their way to make him welcome. We have only to let the Paris ballet know we want to stay in their country. They will go to the authorities for us."

Vera was so convincing, it was hard not to believe her. She was like the ballet we had just danced, full of fire. As long as she was beside me, how could we not succeed?

The next morning Vera was still complaining of her knee and limped into the rehearsal room with it bound so tightly, she had trouble with her *pliés*. Vitaly groaned during his lifts. Madame was cross and impatient. When I casually picked up a towel to mop the sweat from my neck, Marina screeched at me, "Keep your hands off my towel."

"I'd die before I touched your filthy towel," I said, and threw it on the floor.

"Enough!" Madame said. "You are like a room full of kindergartners. If you think such amateurs will be sent to France to represent the Soviet Union during this time of trouble, think again." Madame knew the whole country was in an uproar over the demonstrations. The battle over politics might even put an end to our tour.

At the lunch break Vera, Vitaly, and I huddled together with no appetite for our *pelmeny*. When Aidan joined us, she said, "Everyone is out of sorts. What is going on?"

Vitaly said, "The country is going crazy. Yeltsin's people are planning to demonstrate and Gorbachev is threatening to bring out the police to stop them. Stupid politicians are going to ruin our chance to go to Paris."

"No one can be so stupid as to want the old Stalin days back," I said. Only a few years after my grandfather Georgi had served so bravely in the war, Stalin had sent him and Grandmother into exile for five years, and they were lucky; thousands and thousands of the heroes of the Siege of Leningrad had been executed by Stalin.

Aidan said, "What was so bad about Stalin? When

he was here, my family was thriving in Lithuania. Now I am back in Russia with nothing."

I was furious. "Your family might have been better off, but the whole country of Lithuania had been taken over by Stalin. The Lithuanians only want their freedom back."

Vera said, "Stop all the arguing. What do politics matter? All that matters is having the company go to Paris."

Some of the dancers had gone out to have lunch. They were returning, shedding their coats and hats and changing from boots into toe slippers. I saw Marina sidle up to Madame and hand her a newspaper. I thought nothing of it until at the end of the day Madame called me aside. Her smile was so pained, I thought either her chignon was pulled too tightly or I was having trouble again with my *chassé en tournant*, landing awkwardly after my *tour en l'air*. I had no idea that it was Grandfather Georgi who was giving her such a vexed look.

"Tanya," she said in a confidential voice, "we all admire your grandfather for his service to Leningrad, but if he continues to oppose Gorbachev, he will bring down the country, and that will be the end of the tour as well." She held out *Leningradskaya Pravda* for me to see, and there on the front page of the newspaper was my grandfather with a big sign saying SUPPORT YELTSIN. I felt my face turn red.

Madame said, "President Gorbachev has outlawed the rally. Let's hope our director, Maxim Nikolayevich, does not learn who your grandfather is." With that she stalked away. As I hurried out, I saw Marina laughing with some of the members of the corps.

I was torn in two. I loved and admired Grandfather Georgi. He was the optimist in the family, always the cheerful one who could see the humorous side of anything. Though he recognized Russia's problems, he believed they could be solved. Fighter that he was, he was always ready to risk his life to solve them.

I thought about Grandfather all the way home. When I was a little girl, he would take me on picnics in the Summer Garden and to the wharves to see the ships come in. Every year on the first day of April I would go with Grandfather to see him and his friends shed their clothes down to their bathing trunks and jump into the Neva to go "walrusing," splashing about among the chunks of ice. "The ice is from my Lake Ladoga," he would say. Once he took me to see the monument to the heroic defenders of Leningrad. He told me of his dangerous work riding trucks during the Siege of Leningrad, a time when the Germans had surrounded the city and half a million people died of starvation. With bombs falling all around them, the trucks had rumbled across frozen Lake Ladoga to bring food into the city. Grandfather and I visited Memorial Hall to hear the beat of a metronome. During the siege if there was no news or no music on the radio, a metronome was played so that all would know that the city of Leningrad was still there. I wanted to tell Grandfather to stay out of the newspapers, but knowing him, I had little hope.

At the apartment it was just as I knew it would be. The whole family, along with Aunt Marya, was sitting around the table arguing politics. Grandfather was excited after his day of demonstrating. "If we don't allow Yeltsin to get rid of the collective farms and let people own their own land, we will have famine in this country," Grandfather said. "What's more, Yeltsin will end the coal miners' strike. Gorbachev sits in his fancy country house, built for him by the government at the cost of millions of rubles, doing nothing."

Mama was tumbling slices of carrot and celery into the cabbage soup. "Papa," she said, "the fight isn't just between Yeltsin and Gorbachev. Today on the way home from the hotel I saw Communists carrying signs. They are against letting the people own their own land and businesses. They want to go back to the Stalinist days. One had a sign calling Yeltsin 'tsarist riffraff.'"

Grandfather gave one of his explosive laughs. "Tsarist riffraff! Who will take that seriously?"

"I'll tell you who," Father said. "The soldiers in the army who have been sent back from Poland and Hungary and all the other countries Russia occupied. Those soldiers have been kicked out of the army, and they have no jobs and no food. They want us to march back into Poland and Hungary so they can have their jobs back."

When I heard that, I was sure Vitaly's father was one of those soldiers without jobs. "I'll tell you who won't have a job if her grandfather keeps getting his picture in the paper," I said. I told them how Madame had taken me aside and showed me the article in *Leningradskaya Pravda*.

Mama turned on Grandfather. "There, Papa, you see what all that demonstrating has done to our Tanya."

Grandfather reached for my hand and held it

tightly. "Tanya, my dear, I would give up everything for you, even my life, but one thing I would not give up is freedom for this unhappy country. However, I will promise you that after this, the moment I see a camera I will go the other way."

And with that I had to be satisfied.

CHAPTER 5

THE RESCUE

But Grandfather was Grandfather, and he was sure to be in the thick of any public event. A few days later *Leningradskaya Pravda* had an article about him, showing him and his friends jumping into the Neva for their annual "walrusing." The paper identified Grandfather as one of the supporters of Yeltsin. I dreaded facing Madame. I could hardly drag myself along the streets. The snow had returned, an ugly April snow that melted into slush as soon as it hit the streets. When I entered the rehearsal hall, everyone grew quiet and I was sure they had been talking of me and my accursed family. I thought I might just as well give up the idea of joining the tour to Paris. If there was to be a tour, as the granddaughter of a thorn in President Gorbachev's side I would be nothing but an embarrassment.

Marina gave me a smug smile. Even Vera seemed to keep her distance from me. Madame's expression was more austere than usual. It was Vitaly who said there was a rumor that our director, Maxim Nikolayevich, himself was coming in to rehearse us. I got into my leotard and toe shoes and began to busy myself at the barre doing *battements dégagés* as if my life depended on them. Maxim Nikolayevich stalked into the room wearing a sheepskin coat, a scarf that came down to his ankles, and the look of a man about to break down a door. He set us all to working until we were ready to drop. My ankles gave out, my toes hurt, my instep ached, and still Maxim Nikolayevich drove us, as if, should we let up even for a second, the whole world would end. When at last the rehearsal was over, I saw Madame walking toward me.

"Tanya," Madame said in her most severe voice, "Maxim Nikolayevich wishes to have a word with you."

I stood perfectly still, unable to move. I was sure that for the good of the troupe he would to ask me to leave. I tried to imagine how I would pass my days if I were thrown out of the troupe, but I could not. And then with a disappointment that stopped me in my tracks, I realized that if I could not go to Paris, there would be no chance to defect. Russian politics were going to ruin my dancing career. It was impossible to be a dedicated ballerina in such a country. I decided that if by some miracle I got to go to Paris, I would stay there.

"Tanya," Madame repeated, "pay attention. What is the matter with you? Maxim Nikolayevich has better things to do than wait for you. Go!"

The other dancers pretended not to stare, but every one of them was watching me. I remembered my first lesson in ballet school, when I was six. How to hold my head. I made a little parade of one across the floor to the director. Maxim Nikolayevich was glowering at me.

"Come into the office, Tatiana Ivanova."

The office was a cubbyhole filled with bound volumes of ballet scores, sheets of music, ballet magazines from around the world, and yellowing programs from past performances. On the walls were pictures of Russia's two greatest ballerinas, Pierina Legnani and Mathilde Kschessinska. On the desk were empty cans of soda and a pair of old toe shoes.

Maxim Nikolayevich frowned at me.

"I had a call this morning from someone whose name I will not mention," Maxim Nikolayevich said. "The caller had seen the article in *Ballet* magazine about you, mentioning your family. He also saw the article on your grandfather in *Leningradskaya Pravda*. He did not think it was in the best interests of the country to have you in the troupe. He was especially concerned at the thought that you might go on the tour and be seen as a representative of someone who sympathizes with your grandfather's views. I believe he described them as 'extreme views.'"

How I had shown the magazine article around, how I had boasted about it. Now I saw where my pride had taken me. I cursed the day the magazine had come out.

"Tell, me, Tatiana Ivanova, what do you think of your grandfather?"

Ah, there it was. If I said I thought he was a fool to take the positions he did, if I denounced him as an enemy of the state, perhaps all would be well. "I love my grandfather," I said. "I think he is a great hero."

Suddenly there was a smile on Maxim Nikolaye-vich's face. How could that be? "My thoughts exactly," he said. "I had the pleasure of telling the important man who called me that I was the one who decided who would dance with the troupe and who would go on tour. I have been accused of considering myself the greatest ballet director in Russia and perhaps the world. That is true on two counts. I think it and I am.

I know perfectly well Gorbachev could be replaced, but they cannot replace me. Not a word of this to anyone. Now go back to your *battements dégagés*, and I want to see that working foot higher from the floor." With that Maxim Nikolayevich swept his scarf about his neck and marched out of the office.

When I returned to the rehearsal room, my face was burning. Vera came over and put her arm around me, but the others treated me as if I had a disease they might catch. At lunch the others kept their distance until they saw Vera and Vitaly settle next to me; then, one by one, they joined us. "What did the Great One have to say?" Vera asked.

"Tell us!" Vitaly begged.

"He criticized my *battements dégagés*," I said. "He told me to bring my working foot higher."

They stared incredulously at me. "I don't believe you," Vera said.

"I swear it's true," I said.

The word must have gone around, and Marina

looked daggers at me, for personal criticism from Maxim Nikolayevich was a hundred times better than praise from anyone else. It meant he had *noticed* you.

I carried my little secret with me all day, forcing myself not to smile foolishly as I felt like doing. How I longed to tell someone. As I walked through the streets on my way to the children's shelter, I didn't see the slush or feel the cold. I could only say Maxim Nikolayevich's name over and over to myself as if it were a charm that would protect me from any danger. There was still a chance that should the tour take off for Paris, I would be on the plane. Come summer I might be strolling down the Champs-Élysées.

I was still smiling when I reached the shelter. I was so caught up with my secret that at first I didn't notice the troubled look on Uncle Fyodor's face. "Natalia is gone. We've lost her."

"What happened?"

"Her father has tracked her down. He turned up at the shelter, drunk, demanding that she go home with him. Natalia's mother has left her husband—and why not? He has made her life a misery. The man played on Natalia's sympathies, saying he was sick and had no one to care for him. He went down on his knees. He said he was all alone and had only a few weeks to live. He begged Natalia to come and take care of him. She went."

I was horrified. "Couldn't you stop her?"

Uncle Fyodor shook his head. "How could we? The man is her father."

"Do you think he is really sick?"

"I believe it was all a sham, but what an actor that man would have made. I only wish we had someone in authority we could call on to help Natalia."

"Give me her address," I said.

Uncle Fyodor shook his head. "No, Tanya. I don't want you going there. It's a bad neighborhood and he is a dangerous man."

My pupils had little enthusiasm for their lessons, for they all missed Natalia; still I put them through their paces. Madame always told us there was no sorrow that could not be cured by work. As I left, Yulia pressed a piece of paper into my hand. She whispered, "Natalia and I shared a cupboard. I found a letter from her father there with a return address." I reached for the letter and hid it in my purse. "Will you bring her back, Tanya?"

"I'll try," I promised. When I was away from the shelter, I took out the letter. It was nothing more than a scrawl on a stained piece of paper. "Natalia, your papa needs you. I am dying."

There were some not-so-lovely parts of Leningrad. As I walked among tumbledown gray houses that gave off a hopeless feeling of poverty and despair, I felt I could enter any one of those houses and hear a sad story. The yards were bare and muddy, the only landscaping piles of trash. Skinny dogs pulled on their chains and growled, busy with protecting the little that was left to the families. Ragged children stood at the doorways or poked about in the mud with sticks. As I passed a house, a curtain would twitch at a window and a suspicious face peer out. Any stranger in that neighborhood would be regarded as an enemy. I had nearly lost my courage by the time I found the address.

Natalia's house was nothing more than a shack with four walls and a roof. The two windows that looked out onto the street were barred. A crudely lettered sign said KEEP OUT. I stood there looking at the house, thinking Uncle Fyodor was right and I should turn around and retrace my steps. The front door opened, and Natalia ran out and flung herself at me.

"Tanya, the angels sent you. Come inside so we won't be seen."

"Where is your father?"

"He goes out every afternoon to see friends."

"I thought he was sick."

"He says since I have come home to take care of the house and see that he has meals, he is much better."

I saw a bruise on her arm. "How did you get that?"

"I must have tripped and fallen against something."

"Natalia, you are the most graceful person in the world. I don't see you stumbling about. It was your father, wasn't it?"

Natalia began to cry. "He's not a bad man, but when he gets his pension, he spends it all on vodka and he comes home in a mean mood. If I don't have his supper on the table, he scolds me, but often there's no money for food, so how can I make him supper?"

"Natalia, come back to the shelter with me. Your father is a grown man. He can take care of himself."

"No, you don't understand. He really is sick. He coughs all the time. The vodka is only to make him feel a little better. He says he will die if I go back. Tanya, believe me, he is not all bad. He is discouraged because he can't find a job. When I was a little girl, he would take Mama and me out into the country, and you should have heard him whistle to the birds, so real the birds would whistle back, and once he brought home a little rabbit for me and built a cage for it."

"Natalia, what about your dancing?"

Her eyes filled with tears. "It will have to wait."

"It can't wait. You are already old to start ballet school. The lessons from me are not enough. Let me talk with Madame about you and ask her to give you an audition. Listen to me, Natalia. I truly believe you have it in you to be a great ballerina, and artists in this country must make use of their talents. They have a responsibility to be the best they can. Great art will always lead to freedom, the freedom that so many people in our country died for." All the while I was trying to convince Natalia of her responsibility to Russia, I was guiltily thinking how I would soon be deserting my country. My words stuck in my throat.

The door banged as if a strong wind had blown it open. A man, who I guessed was Natalia's father, stormed into the room. He stared at me as if I were a bit of food that had gone bad. "Who are you?" he demanded. "Someone come to steal my daughter?"

"I'm not trying to steal her, but I think she should come back to the shelter and her dancing."

"She's going nowhere. She is my daughter, and it is up to her to take care of me in my dying days."

"You look healthy to me."

My words infuriated him. "Who are you to tell me how I feel? You have probably never been sick a day in your life or wanted for food on the table. How can you come here and try to separate a father from his daughter?" He turned to Natalia. "Tell the girl you don't want to leave your old, sick dad."

Natalia looked helplessly at me. Earlier in the day I had stuck by my grandfather when he was attacked. Why should Natalia not stick by her father? Who was I to interfere?

"Now get out of here. We have company coming tonight for supper, and Natalia must prepare the food."

Reluctantly I began to leave. As I was going out the door, I saw the father put a bag of potatoes, a cabbage, and a thick slab of meat on the table. There was a bottle of wine as well.

Natalia stared at the food in wonder. "Papa, where did all that come from?" Curious, I lingered at the door.

Natalia's father swung around and gave me a rough push. "We want you out of here." He slammed the door after me, but I stood there listening. The wood was so thin, I could hear everything.

"Have you robbed a store?" Natalia asked.

"Shame on you. What kind of a daughter are you to accuse me of such a thing? The gentleman who is coming for dinner has paid for our food. It will be your job to be nice to the man, and maybe he will give us more than food."

I ran off. Uncle Fyodor was right. The father would stop at nothing. Natalia's beauty and natural grace, which would help to make her a great ballerina, meant nothing more to her father than a way to make money. I knew I could not do anything by myself, and the police were so few and so busy they would never listen to me. I needed someone to help me. I thought of Uncle Fyodor, but he was a man of peace, not action. I considered my father, but he always had to think on all sides of a question. By the time he had his answer, it would be too late. I considered Sasha, but with his grandmother's illness, he had all he could manage. There was only Grandfather.

I rushed breathless into the apartment and began to tug at Grandfather, signaling him that I wanted him out in the hall. Any word in the apartment was overhead by all.

"Tanya, what is wrong with you?" he said. "You are as bad as the riot police. Next you will go after me with a bludgeon and tear gas."

"I have to talk with you," I said.

By now I had the attention of Mama and Grandmother. "Tanya, dear, what is it?" Grandmother said. "Surely you can talk in front of us."

I blurted out my story.

"What are you thinking?" Mama said. "The man is dangerous. It would be madness for your grand-father to tackle him alone."

Grandfather was already hurrying toward the bedroom. He called over his shoulder, "You say he was in the army? I have a plan."

Minutes later he returned, struggling into the jacket of his old Red Army uniform, a uniform he put on each year for the May 9 victory parade. Grandfather, who never stood still for more than a minute, was still in fine shape, and the jacket, though a little tight around the stomach after forty-five years, still fit him. "Let us hope the man is so drunk, he will not notice that my uniform is an old one."

When Grandfather put on his military cap and threw out his chest, he looked very impressive. He had even pinned on some of his medals, which he always kept shined.

Mother and Grandmother followed us out the

door calling words of caution to us all the way down the stairway. The last thing we heard was Mama's plea: "Papa, think what you are doing. Come back!" Grandfather only hurried the faster. I knew that he was eager to help Natalia, but I could also see his uniform had brought back memories, and now he was not only ready but anxious for one more battle. I began to have hope for Natalia.

We marched through the streets, Grandfather far in front of me. It was dark now. The cars caught us in their headlights as we hurried along. People nervously gave way as Grandfather plowed through the crowds as if he were on some official mission. When we reached Natalia's house, Grandfather slowed and began cautiously to approach the window, motioning me to stay back, but I stayed right behind him.

"Grandfather," I whispered, "that's Natalia crying."

The next minute Grandfather was kicking in the front door. Natalia's father and another man were sitting at a table, a bottle of vodka in front of them, the remains of their dinner on the plates, the wine bottle empty. Natalia's father had her by the arm. As they rose to their feet, Natalia escaped and ran toward me.

In a loud authoritarian voice Grandfather shouted, "Pyotr Vasilyevich, the army has sent me to tell you that your behavior is such that your pension will be withdrawn."

Natalia's father cringed. "Withdrawn? What for? How will I live?"

The other man said, "Shut up, Pyotr Vasilyevich." He turned to Grandfather. "I am sure this is just a misunderstanding. We are all friends here. Have a little glass of vodka with us and let us see if we can't find a way to compensate you for your trouble in coming here."

Grandfather reached over and slammed the bottle of vodka against the table, breaking it in two and splashing the liquor over the startled man. He grabbed

the man by the shoulders and shook him. "Get out!"
Grandfather thundered. The man hastily scuttled out
of the room.

Grandfather turned to Natalia's father. "Pyotr
Vasilyevich, I know what you are up to, selling your
own daughter. For that you could not only lose your
pension, but be put away for a dozen years. For the
sake of your daughter I won't turn you in, but you
must promise never again to approach Natalia or to
communicate with her." Grandfather strode out of the
house, Natalia on one arm and me on the other.

Once we were back at the shelter, with Uncle
Fyodor pouring out hot tea for us, Natalia told us her
story. "I didn't understand at first," she said. "I
thought the man who gave us the food was just kind-
hearted. I even fixed up the house a little, dusting and
putting out dishes with no chips or cracks so that we
would not be ashamed in front of the man. Of course
I should have known better, but I wanted more than

anything to trust Papa. It's hard to admit to yourself that your father is an evil man.

"The man brought a bottle of vodka with him, and I saw him give Papa some rubles. By the time I had dinner on the table, Papa and the man were drunk. The man began to put his paws on me, calling me his pretty princess. When I slapped his hand away, Papa said that was no way to act toward a friend. I tried to get away, but Papa hung on to me. I was frightened and started to cry, but Papa only hung on harder. That was when you came." She turned to Grandfather. "What kind of soldier are you?"

Grandfather laughed. "I belong to a special branch of the army organized just to carry out Tanya's orders."

"Whatever kind of soldier you are, you saved me, but I can't stay here in the shelter. I'm even afraid to stay in this city," Natalia said. "I don't care what Papa promised about not seeing me again. I know him. He will hunt me down. I have to run away."

"Natalia," I said, "I have a better idea. Your father won't dare to show up at the shelter tonight. Wait here until tomorrow."

CHAPTER 6

☐ CONFESSION

The next morning at the first break during rehearsal, I approached Madame. She had been in a good mood, hardly scolding us at all and even complimenting Aidan on her playing, telling us the accompanist was not there just to pound out tunes, but to put her soul into the music as we must put our souls into our dancing.

Taking a deep breath, I asked, "Madame, can I have a word with you?" I told her Natalia's story, leaving out the part about Grandfather and his uniform, telling her only that Natalia had been rescued and needed to get away from Leningrad. "Please let me bring her here and show you how she can dance. She should be in a ballet school."

"You say she is twelve and has no formal training. It's much too late for her."

"I've been trying to teach her for over a year, but whatever you decide, just think of her miserable life, Madame; think how much it would mean to her to have the chance to dance just this once for the great Pleshakova."

Madame shrugged. "Well, nothing will come of it, but bring her by this afternoon."

Natalia was so nervous when I gave her the news that at first she refused. "I couldn't. She will laugh at my clumsiness."

"Natalia, this is your one chance. Madame will be truthful, but I promise she won't laugh."

Mercifully, except for Aidan, Madame and I were the only ones in the rehearsal hall to witness the audition. Self-consciously Natalia warmed up at the barre. I explained to Aidan the little ballet I had devised for

Natalia from *The Red Shoes*.

"Yes, yes, I know the story," Aidan said, and began to play, nodding her head at Natalia. Natalia paused in the third position as if waiting for the lifting of some spell that would free her to dance. For a moment I was afraid she had been overcome with shyness and had panicked. She was staring at Aidan. I realized that never in her life had she heard music coming from a human being. At the shelter I played records, and when in her miserable life had someone taken her to a concert or a live performance of ballet? The music enchanted her, turning her into a statue.

Aidan changed the tempo of the music. It became more lively. Suddenly Natalia began to dance as if she had studied a secret language for years and now, at last, was allowed to speak it. There were *fouettés*, *échappés*, *jetés*, *battements frappés*, *demi-pliés*, and *relevés*. She was using every step I had ever taught her, many I recalled illustrating only once to show the variety of steps. The music had become her red slippers. As long as Aidan played, Natalia had to dance. I was both excited and a little envious. Though I knew I danced well, better than most, Natalia danced as if she were jumping from a tall diving board, with no thought to what might catch her.

When at last Aidan stopped, Natalia's arms dropped and her feet came to rest in a perfect fifth position. I saw Madame hastily brush tears from her eyes. "I have a friend who is ballet mistress at the Bolshoi Ballet," Madame said. "She will find a ballet school for you. I will call her at once. Tomorrow you will be on the train to Moscow."

Natalia flung her arms around me. She then had the courage to do what none of us would have imagined doing. She threw her arms around Madame and danced her about. Madame only pretended to be displeased.

A week later I had a letter from Moscow. Natalia was in ballet school. Her spelling was like her dancing, wild and full of invention, but it was plain that she was in heaven. She wrote, "I O you my life."

Spring settled on the city. Without coats and boots I felt light enough to float up into the clouds. The wooden boxes were removed from the statues in the Summer Garden, and the Roman emperors and voluptuous women were once again set free. It was the time of the white nights in our northern city—the long June evenings had arrived, when the sun seemed only to fade and never to set. I had seen little of Sasha, for we were practicing long hours on a new presentation of Ravel's *Bolero* and Sasha, desperate for money for his grandmother, was working day and night at his icons. When at last I had a few hours off, I dragged Sasha from his apartment. "Come with me to the Hermitage," I said. "You need some inspiration." Though I had missed seeing Sasha, I knew that he was nearby; what would it be like when I was a thousand miles away?

Walking along the Prospekt, Sasha turned his face

up to the sun, as if some cold thing within him needed warming. Though it was June, you could still see chunks of ice floating down the river from Lake Ladoga miles away. Our city is made up of many islands. With all its rivers and canals there is always danger of flooding from the spring melt. This year the Neva was keeping tidily to its banks.

Sasha said, "People walk through the city, hurrying to get somewhere, missing everything. Look there on the canal, a perfect reflection of the Church of the Resurrection."

It was true. The church's reflection, with its brightly colored domes, looked as real as the one that stood solidly on the ground.

"There are two cities, Tanya, one that can be touched and the city that is reflected in the canals and rivers. The city I like to paint is the one that is there one moment and gone the next with a ripple of water or a cloud passing by. The great thing about painting is that if you see something you like, you can make it your own to keep forever."

"Unlike a dance," I said.

"No, no," Sasha reassured me. "I am learning to paint movement. I can capture a dance as well as a reflection."

I thought of all his sketches of the ballet and had to admit he was right. I was not sure, though, that even he could have caught Natalia's dancing.

We walked across Palace Square, which is very famous for Bloody Sunday. A hundred years ago the tsar's soldiers opened fire on people who had come to ask for a voice in the government. Even women and little children had been killed. Now there was always something cheerful going on in the square. Four students, dressed in mismatched evening clothes, were playing their string instruments. They fiddled away, hair tossing about, earnest expressions on their faces, looking as if they were in a great concert hall. A kettle was in front of them for coins. Sasha emptied his pockets. Nearby was a man with a trained bear cub on a chain. The cub looked like a stuffed toy. The man had a kettle as well, and this time I emptied my pockets.

In the middle of the square the Alexander column celebrated Russia's victory over Napoleon. At the top of the column the golden angel watched over our city. Across the square was the Winter Palace, painted sea green and trimmed with white and gold. A row of statues looked down from the roof where during the Great Patriotic War my grandmother Yelena was a fire warden. The palace was now the Hermitage Museum.

At the Hermitage I asked Sasha to come with me to Aunt Marya's office. Sasha liked her as much as I did and came willingly. "How I envy your aunt," he said. "She has been to Paris and has wandered through the Louvre. What wouldn't I give to see that museum. If I were rich, I would buy postcards of every painting that hangs there."

I longed to tell Sasha that by the fall I would be

settled in Paris and could send him all the postcards he wished from the Louvre, but I had pledged my vow of silence to Vera.

In Aunt Marya's office there was an older man talking away to her. He was so short, he came only to Aunt Marya's shoulder. The man had thick white hair, bright-blue eyes, and a mischievous grin that made him look half elf, half man. Aunt Marya kissed us and said, "The very two people I wanted to see. This is Mr. Brompton. He comes from England. He is here to find some paintings for his London gallery. When I heard he was looking for the work of young artists, I thought of you at once, Sasha. You must take him to see your work and give him the names of some of your fellow artists."

Sasha was elated. "Gladly. When do you want to come, sir?"

"Now is as good a time as any," Mr. Brompton said. He turned to Aunt Marya. "If you will allow me to come back later, I will hold you to your promise to show me through the museum."

Sasha seemed overwhelmed by the sudden turn of events. He looked to me for support. "Tanya, you come too. It always cheers Grandmother to see you." To Mr. Brompton he said, "My work isn't in any gallery—it only hangs on the walls of our small room."

Mr. Brompton gave Sasha a reassuring pat on the back. "A painting is a painting, never mind where it hangs. I have an eye for quality."

Mr. Brompton had a car and a driver at his disposal, so much to our delight we were driven to Sasha's apartment, Sasha in the front seat and me in back with Mr. Brompton. I stumbled along in English until we found we both spoke French. What a feeling of luxury to be driven down the Prospekt in a fancy car. I had visions of the Empress Alexandra and Tsar Nicholas making their way along the Prospekt in their golden coach.

Sasha hurried into the apartment and drew the curtain across his work area with its icons. I knew he was ashamed of spending so much time copying old work when he should have been creating his own pictures.

When I saw Sasha's grandmother, my heart felt as cold as the lumps of ice in the Neva. Nadya Petrovna had grown thinner and paler, and now she nearly disappeared into the bedcovers. When I took her hand in mine, it was like holding a shadow.

Sasha introduced his grandmother to Mr. Brompton, who was extremely charming to her, bowing over her thin, trembling hand as if he might kiss it, but all the while his eyes were scanning the walls. "Ah, Sasha, I must have some of those ballet sketches and paintings you have done. I know I can sell them." He looked more closely at me. "And here is the subject of many of them. Very charming. Pictures of the ballet always sell." Sasha was beaming, hanging on the man's every word.

Nadya Petrovna said, "Sasha, where are your manners? You must make some tea for our guests."

While Sasha was busy with the kettle, I watched Mr. Brompton. All his attention was on the icon of St. Vladimir. He turned to Nadya Petrovna. "That is a very old one, is it not?"

"Oh, yes," Nadya Petrovna said. "It has belonged to our family for many years and to a very special family before that."

"I could get you a great deal of money for your icon," Mr. Brompton said.

Sasha, walking in with the tea, overheard his remark. Before Sasha could say anything, Nadya Petrovna said, "Oh, I would never sell St. Vladimir. It would be like selling my own father. St. Vladimir is all that keeps me alive."

I didn't like the greedy look on the man's face. "Isn't it against the law to take old icons out of the country?" I asked.

"Yes, yes," Mr. Brompton said, "but one can get around that. You only have to give a little money to the right person." He gave a regretful look at the icon and then turned to Sasha. "Of course I can't pay you for your paintings until my gallery sells them, which might take a little time."

Sasha looked crestfallen, but he shrugged his shoulders. "No one has money for paintings in this country, so I may as well send them with you and hope for the best."

"I'm sure I can manage a little advance to help you out," Mr. Brompton said, and Sasha brightened.

After we had finished the tea, Mr. Brompton said a polite farewell to Nadya Petrovna, looked longingly again at the icon, and began to leave. Sasha said, "Wait a moment and I'll walk down the stairway with you." He turned to me. "Keep Grandmother company, Tanya. I'll be only a moment."

He was gone for some time, and when he returned his face was burning. He wouldn't look at me or at Nadya Petrovna and only said, "I'll call you in a few days, Tanya."

That night Aunt Marya stopped by. As usual the

family was sitting around the kitchen table drinking tea and arguing politics. Gorbachev was in Sweden receiving the Nobel Prize. Grandfather was furious. "A peace prize to a man who just months ago sent his tanks and soldiers to trample freedom in Lithuania."

Grandmother said, "At least he allowed the wall to fall in Berlin."

"Only because he was goaded into it," Grandfather sneered. The American president, Ronald Reagan, had challenged, "President Gorbachev, take down that wall!"

Grandfather had been celebrating all week, for Yeltsin had been elected to the presidency of Russia. "At last we will see some action," Grandfather said.

Aunt Marya was Grandfather's older sister and never let an opportunity go by without reminding him of that. She said, "Don't think, Georgi, that all our problems are solved. I have heard rumors everywhere that the Communist party leaders are furious with Yeltsin. They know he wants to dissolve the party and that would be the end of them."

Mother gave Aunt Marya a cup of tea, and after taking a sip, Aunt Marya said, "I didn't come here to argue politics with you, Georgi. I came to have a word with Tanya. I wanted to tell you, Tanya: I don't trust that Mr. Brompton. I took him about the museum, where he had a greedy eye for everything he saw. I told him it was no longer like it was under Stalin, when our birthright was snatched from under us and some of our very best works of art were sold to the United States. I think you should warn Sasha to take care."

"He wants some of Sasha's paintings to sell in his gallery," I said. "He is giving Sasha a small advance, but the rest of the money won't come to Sasha until his work is sold."

"Tell Sasha not to give him too much and certainly not his best things. I think he is here only to make a grab for our treasures, not to further the work of young Russian artists as he professes."

It was a week later that Mama sent me with some

jars of her strawberry jam to Sasha's grandmother. Nadya Petrovna was sitting up in an armchair, a bright shawl around her shoulders, Kuzma chirping in his cage, the teakettle steaming, Sasha at his easel painting one of his icons. The moment I walked into the room, Sasha hastily covered up the icon. No one looks more guilty when he does something wrong than Sasha. His cheeks burn and he drops his eyes and will not look at you. I did not have to wait long to find out what was on his canvas. Before he could interrupt her, Nadya Petrovna said in her soft whispery voice, "My grandson is a saint. Just see what he is painting. A copy of the icon of St. Vladimir. He tells me a church has ordered it, and the church must be paying well, for Sasha has brought home some special medicine for me. Already I'm feeling better." She eagerly tasted the jam I had brought, declaring it the best ever.

"Sasha," I said, "what good luck. Tell me the name of the church." A few of the churches that had been closed by the government were once again opening their doors.

"You have never heard of it," he said quickly. "There's no time for chatter. Come and help me get the laundry and bed linen together. I have a friend who has promised me the use of his washing machine for an hour if I come at once. Keep Grandmother company while I'm gone."

After he left, I cleaned Kuzma's cage and tidied the small room. Before I was finished, Nadya Petrovna drifted off to sleep. My curiosity got the better of me. I lifted the cover from the painting. The icon of St. Vladimir was identical to his grandmother's icon, but unlike the other icons Sasha painted, which were meant to look old but which you could tell with a little studying were reproductions, this one was different. Sasha was painting this one to look authentic: the colors faded, the gold dark with age. Perhaps, I thought, that's the way the church wants it to look.

But would a church want to fool people? I remembered Sasha's guilty look.

When he came back, his arms full of sheets and towels, all tumbled together, I was waiting for him. I pulled him outside the apartment and closed the door. I whispered, "You're going to sell that icon to Mr. Brompton and pretend it's the original."

"What if I am?"

"That's dishonest."

"I don't care. Brompton has given me the advance for my paintings, and I was able to get Grandmother the medicine she needs. See how much better she is already."

"Your grandmother would rather die than have you steal and end up in jail."

"You didn't tell her!"

"Of course not. What do you take me for? But you have to stop at once."

"Not as long as I need the money. If he is stupid

enough to buy it, let him." Sasha gave me a furious look. "If you're just going to stand here and lecture me, you can go home. I don't want to hear your holier-than-thou accusations."

He looked so miserable, I put an arm around him. "Sasha, there has to be a better way to get money."

"Then go and find it." He pulled away from me and disappeared into the apartment. I heard his grandmother asking if I had left. "Yes," he said. "Tanya left a while ago."

"Such a nice girl, Sasha. I like to see the two of you together."

Crossly Sasha answered, "I'd be happier with Tanya if she weren't always telling me what to do."

With his hurtful words in my head I hurried off. Only a week before, I had told Vera how much Sasha needed money for medicine, thinking her family might help, but Vera had shaken her head. "Things have gotten hard at home. Since Yeltsin was elected president, he is making it difficult for Papa." Hard as I tried, I could think of no other way for Sasha to get money.

I followed the Neva to the bridge that leads to the railroad station where trains departed for Finland. Though I had never been on a train, I loved to watch passengers depart and to imagine that like them I was traveling to some distant country. In front of the station was a huge statue of Lenin, his arm stretched out in a kind of salute. People made a joke of it and said he was hailing a taxi. Grandfather would not let us turn Lenin into a joke. "He has the blood of Russians on his hands," he said. "It is not a laughing matter."

I wandered back though the Summer Garden, where hundreds of scarlet geraniums bloomed like a field of red soldiers. Even the fragrance of the lilac bushes could not cheer me. I knew there were severe penalties if an artist were caught faking old icons and selling them for the real thing. If Sasha were put in jail, there would be no medicine for his grandmother and no one to care for her.

MAKING TROUBLE FOR GREGORY

The next morning when we entered the practice room, there was a feeling of suspense in the air. We guessed that at last we would hear the news we had been waiting for. Maxim Nikolayevich gathered the entire ballet troupe together to tell us that the tour would be going to Paris in August. "First we will take the train to Moscow, where we will stay for two days. That will give us an opportunity to attend a performance of the Bolshoi. We will see how ballet is meant to be performed." Maxim Nikolayevich gave us a wicked smile, for the competition between our Kirov Ballet and Moscow's Bolshoi Ballet was legendary. Maxim

Nikolayevich would have fought anyone who suggested we were not better than the Bolshoi.

"Unfortunately," he told us, "we will not be able to take the entire troupe. That makes me very sad, but remember this: Although all of you will not go, your hearts will go with us and will help us to give a performance that will bring Paris to its knees. As for those of you who are going, in the next months you will curse your fate, for you will work until you wish you had never been chosen. If it is a question of working you to death or giving a mediocre performance, you will be worked to death. Depend upon it."

That afternoon the list of the lucky ones who would go on the tour was posted. As we jostled one another to read the list, there were cries of joy and tears. My name was on the list, and so were Vera's and Marina's, but Vitaly's name was not there. Before we could comfort him, he ran out of the practice hall. I ran after him, but he called over his shoulder, "Just leave me alone."

We had known a choice would have to be made between Vitaly and Gregory, but we had all been sure Vitaly would be chosen, for he was clearly the better dancer. If talent had been the criterion, Vitaly would be going to Paris, but Gregory had started a malicious rumor. He had whispered to Madame that Vitaly was negotiating secretly to join the Bolshoi in Moscow. Of course there was no truth to the rumor, but Madame believed Gregory because he flattered her shamelessly, begging her to tell him stories of the days when she had been a ballerina. He would coax her to bring out her scrapbook with its clippings of her performances. "You must have had lovers by the dozens," he would tease Madame, and she would blush. When Madame was out of sight, Gregory would make fun of her, calling her an "old cow." We guessed that Madame, who had a weakness for flattery, had believed the rumor. Thinking that Vitaly would use his trip to Paris only as leverage to join our rival, the Bolshoi, Madame would have backed Gregory over Vitaly. We all thought it unfair; even Marina whispered to me before the evening's performance of *Romeo and Juliet*, "I've a notion to give the little rat some trouble tonight."

As excited as Vera and I were over our good fortune, we felt bad for Vitaly and for everyone who wouldn't be on that plane to Paris, but our own joy spilled over onto everything. We dug up copies of our French-language textbooks and spoke only French to each other. We hung out in the bookstores reading the fashion magazines and hopelessly comparing what we saw in the magazines with our own clothes, trying to figure out how we could turn them into something Parisian. Aunt Marya, who kept bumping into Vera and me among the French Impressionists at the Hermitage, complimented us on our new interest in art.

We did not allow ourselves to think of what Madame would say if she knew of our treachery. We were not planning to leave the Kirov for the Bolshoi; we were planning to leave Russia altogether.

I began to look at my family in a different way. I had always taken them for granted, as if they would always be there. Now I realized I would soon be leaving them, perhaps forever. Under Yeltsin more travel was allowed, but no one in my family could afford a trip to Paris, and if I ran away from the ballet, I knew I would not be welcomed back into Russia. I watched Mama in the mornings as she dressed in her maid's uniform, arranging her long hair into a neat knot, putting on ugly shoes that would be comfortable for the long hours she worked in the hotel. I saw Papa come home late at night because there was a shortage of doctors at the hospital. After a fourteen-hour day he would slump down at the table while Mama fixed him tea. I would miss Grandmother in her corner of the apartment, typing poems on her ancient typewriter.

And how would I get along without Grandfather? I could hear him say, "What! Run away from your country just to live in the decadent West? You will sell your Russian soul for a television and a pretty dress.

That is not the way of the Gnedich family. We have laid down our lives for our country." When those words popped up in my head, I was ashamed, and only Vera's reminder of the magic city that lay ahead of us and my own determination that leaving Russia would be better for my dancing career kept me from changing my mind.

Soon there was no time to think about what it would be like to leave my family and my country forever. Maxim Nikolayevich had employed a new choreographer, so we had additional routines to learn. As soon as we had mastered a routine and performed it, the trouble would begin. Maxim Nikolayevich would shout and stamp his feet and tell us how miserable our performance was and how he would be ashamed to take us to Paris or indeed, because of our clumsiness, to the smallest country village in Russia. Back we would go to our practice sessions, which now lasted from dawn to dusk—and dusk in Leningrad's July was all night.

We lost weight. The towels we kept around our necks to catch the sweat never had time to dry. We wore out a pair of shoes a day. At night we soaked in the tub to ease our sprains and pulled muscles. Every toe had a bandage. At each practice session at least one person would break down in tears. Sometimes we took our frustration out on one another. Yet there were times when everything came together and all the laws of gravity were broken. We soared, we fell into the music and made it our own, and then even Maxim Nikolayevich allowed himself a small smile.

During the excitement Vitaly had grown strangely quiet. He seldom joined us for lunch, and at the end of practice he hurried away. I tried to talk with him, but he ignored me. One day when he and I were alone together in the cloakroom, I noticed that on top of Vitaly's tote bag were two more bags stuffed to bursting.

"Vitaly, why do you have all your things piled up like that? Is your family moving?"

He started to walk away, but his expression of hurt troubled me. I realized I had been so preoccupied with my own excitement that I had put Vitaly's unhappiness out of my head. I grabbed his arm. "Hey, Vitaly, it's me, Tanya, your friend. Don't run away."

Vitaly sank down onto the floor and I settled next to him, my arm around his shoulder. In a choked voice he said, "I'm going to join a dance group planning to tour Siberia. Siberia isn't Paris, but it gets me away from home, where they don't want to see my face."

"Siberia! That's impossible! You can't be serious. How could you give up your career here? This is the greatest ballet company in the world."

"First of all," Vitaly said, "the greatest ballet company in the world doesn't care what happens to me. Second, they kicked me out at home. If I join this troupe, even if it's going to Siberia, I'll have a roof over my head."

"What do you mean you've been kicked out at home?"

"The Old Soldier always hated the idea of my dancing, but when it looked like I was going with the troupe to France, and when my father actually saw an article about the tour in the paper, he started bragging about me to his friends. Now that I'm not going, my father is finished with me. He told me I must be no good, a failure. We had a fight and he threw me out. A friend will put me up until the end of the month, and then I'll take off with the Siberian tour."

"Vitaly, promise me you won't sign anything. I have an idea. Give me a few days."

He shrugged. "What can you do, Tanya? You mean well, but Gregory is going to Paris and I'm not. That's all that matters."

"Vitaly, trust me for just a few days."

I waited until Marina was by herself and then hurriedly said, "Listen, I have to talk with you."

"Go ahead and talk." She looked at me with suspicion as I led her off to a hallway where we wouldn't be seen.

"It's about Vitaly. His dad has kicked him out because he didn't make the Paris tour. Now Vitaly is going to run off with some second-rate dance group and bury himself in Siberia."

"That's insane," Marina said. "It will be the end of his career. It's all because of that miserable thief, Gregory Ivanovich, and his vicious rumor. How I would like to tear him to bits. He never loses a chance to upstage me. He manages all the lifts so that they end with him facing the audience perfectly composed and me any which way."

"I know," I said. "It's the same with me. Look, what if in my performance tonight and yours tomorrow he should stumble a little, maybe even fall? If it happened with just one of us it would be suspect, but if it happened with both of us, Maxim Nikolayevich would pay attention. Everyone knows there is no love lost between you and me, so no one would dream we would plot something together."

Marina stared at me and then a sly smile broke out

on her face. "Why shouldn't he get what he deserves?"

In the *pas de deux* that evening, as Gregory lifted me, I shifted my weight, leaning just enough to the right to destroy his balance. He listed like a crippled ship to the left, nearly falling. As he lowered me to the ground, he hissed through tight lips, "You clumsy cow."

"Sorry," I whispered, and danced away.

Afterward Maxim Nikolayevich was furious with Gregory. "You looked like a first-year student. Were you asleep?"

"It was Tanya's fault," he said. "She shifted her weight. It was like dancing with a bag of beans."

Maxim Nikolayevich looked at me. "If it makes him feel better," I said, "let him blame me."

The next night *Romeo and Juliet* was performed with Marina as Juliet. Gregory snarled at me, "At least tonight I won't have to dance with an elephant."

"Cow, elephant, make up your mind, Gregory."

"Don't think I don't know what you are up to,

Tanya. You are trying to get Vitaly back with the tour, but you don't have a chance. He's finished. Just watch me tonight with Marina."

As the first notes of the introduction ended in the orchestra, Marina leered at me. Loud enough for everyone backstage to hear she said, "If you want to have a lesson in how a *pas de deux* is danced, watch us tonight."

My heart sank. What if she had agreed to our plan just to make me look bad? I was onstage with the other members of the corps when Gregory and Marina began the *pas de deux*. During the *enlèvement* I was only a few feet away when Gregory fell. I had no idea how Marina managed it. You could hear the audience gasp. Gregory was so shocked to find himself sprawled on the stage floor that, instead of an immediate graceful recovery, he lay there for whole seconds, unable to believe what had happened. I could hear Maxim Nikolayevich from the wings spit out, "Get up, you fool."

When the curtain came down for intermission, Gregory was crying with rage like a two-year-old. "Marina did it on purpose," he shouted.

"Shut up," Maxim Nikolayevich said. "Do you want the audience to hear you? With you it is always someone else's fault. Last night it was Tanya and tonight it is Marina. When will you take responsibility for your own bungling?" Maxim Nikolayevich sought out Vitaly. "Come and talk with me after the performance tonight," he said.

I didn't dare be seen waiting in the dressing rooms for Vitaly. On my way out Marina gave me the briefest of glances, and I saw the corner of one side of her mouth turn up in a wink of a smile. It was such a complicit smile, saying we were friends in arms, that at last I saw my feud with her was over.

I walked slowly down the street and was not at all surprised when I felt two arms grab me from behind and begin to lift me in the air. "Up you go, my clumsy love." Passersby stopped and stared as Vitaly twirled me around and let me down to kiss me on both cheeks. "Maxim Nikolayevich said I am to go on the tour. He said he couldn't take a chance with Gregory. Wait until I tell the Old Soldier."

CHAPTER 8

SAVING SASHA

The next evening Aunt Marya dropped by the apartment after dinner to see what everyone was up to. She was always restless during the white nights. "So much daylight," she said, "it's as if you have to lead two lives instead of one. It exhausts me." Gratefully she accepted the lemonade Mama had made from some powder she had found in the store. Aunt Marya made a face. "Svetlana, this tastes like a dissolved aspirin tablet."

I could see politics were coming and I wanted to escape, but before I got to the door, Aunt Marya said, "Tanya, I saw Mr. Brompton today. He came to say good-bye. He leaves for England tomorrow. I gather he was successful. He looked like the cat that ate the cream. Did Sasha give him some of his paintings to sell?"

"Yes, he took three or four." I said nothing about the icon that Sasha meant to sell him, but I wondered if that was the reason for Mr. Brompton's satisfied look.

"I have been hearing even more unpleasant things about him from artists he has talked into giving him work with no compensation," Aunt Marya said. "Of course it is not unusual for a dealer to wait until he sells a work to give money to an artist, but when the dealer is a thousand miles away, what is an artist to do if he is cheated?"

Hearing the word *cheated*, I realized I had been so busy these last days, I had forgotten all about Sasha and the dangerous, wicked thing he was doing. If Mr. Brompton was dishonest, so was Sasha, even if he was doing it for his grandmother. If I was truly Sasha's friend, I ought to stop him before it was too late. Then I asked the question I had asked myself a hundred times: Was Sasha just a friend or something else? How much did I care for Sasha? In books and movies young men and women went out on dates, going to restaurants and strolling through parks, gradually discovering they were in love. The truth was that between my dancing and Sasha's painting there was no time to find out how we felt about each other, and now with me leaving we might never know.

Aunt Marya was watching me. "Tanya, what is it? Something is worrying you." I longed to tell Aunt Marya what Sasha was doing, but I couldn't give away his secret. "It's only the pressure of getting ready for the tour. Madame and Maxim Nikolayevich expect the impossible." Hastily I excused myself. "I have to pick up a new leotard before the stores close."

As soon as I escaped, I was on my way to Sasha's. Nadya Petrovna greeted me as warmly as ever, but there were tears in her eyes. Her hand when it reached for mine was as spare as one of Kuzma's claws. "Ah, Tanya, you have come just at the right moment. Sasha has been in a terrible mood all day. He spends too much time here in the apartment. He has been working on his icon for the church night and day, and now that it is finished, he doesn't know what to do with himself. Be a good girl and take him out for a walk so that I can have a few minutes of peace."

It was exactly what I meant to do, for I wanted to warn him about Mr. Brompton, but Sasha said, "I can't go out. I have an appointment in another hour to deliver the icon to the church." I saw a neatly wrapped parcel tied with string lying on the table. I wanted to snatch it up and throw it away. Sasha saw the look on my face. "Besides, Tanya doesn't want to spend time with me."

Hastily I said, "Yes, I do. Come with me for a short walk. It's lovely out and as bright as noon."

Nadya Petrovna urged, "Yes, yes, go along, Sasha."

Reluctantly Sasha followed me out of the apartment. The streets were crowded with strollers with no other purpose than to escape tiny rooms and to breathe in the summer air. The people who remained in their apartments had opened wide their windows, and the sounds of radios—and in the larger, more expensive apartments the chatter from televisions—spilled out into the streets. The kiosks were selling ice cream, and little children hung on to their parents with one hand and with the other clutched a dripping ice cream cone. I led Sasha to the little park in front of the Russian Museum, which was close to his apartment. "Sasha, sit down. I must talk to you."

Sasha gave me a sulky look and settled onto a bench. During the Siege of Leningrad the trees had been cut down, for people were desperate for wood to burn to keep themselves from freezing. Even the bark of the trees had been ground up and mixed with flour to make bread. After the end of the Great Patriotic War new trees were planted. Now, after nearly fifty years, they stood tall and made large pools of shade. "Listen, Sasha, Aunt Marya came by this evening. She doesn't trust your Mr. Brompton."

"Why is he *my* Mr. Brompton? I met him through your aunt."

"If she knew what you are doing, she would feel terrible about introducing him to you. Sasha, what if he learns you have cheated him?"

"He is too stupid and greedy. He'll never be able to tell the difference. I had the original right before me. What can he do? He can't call in the police, because it is illegal to buy an old icon. Anyhow, he has already cheated some of my friends. He took their paintings, promising to give them a bit of money as an advance, as he gave me. Now that he has their paintings, he says he will send the money when he gets to England. Even if he sells our paintings, I doubt we will ever see any money."

"Just because he is a cheat doesn't mean you should cheat him."

"Don't lecture me, Tanya. At least he will not be taking a real icon with him." He looked in the direction of the Russian Museum, where the famous icon *Angel Goldhair* was on display. It was eight hundred years old, and thousands had proclaimed that it worked miracles for them. I hoped it was watching over Sasha.

Sasha was pale, his lips a thin line. I saw what it was costing him to sell his soul for the medicine. When I saw how guilty he felt, I took his hand. "Sasha, I'll tell you a secret. When the troupe gets to Paris, Vera and I are going to stay there. I can send you medicine from France. Only wait a few months. Tell the man you have changed your mind."

Sasha was staring at me. "Tanya! I don't believe you. You are lecturing me on cheating and look what you plan to do—cheat the ballet that has trained you and made you the fine ballerina you are."

I felt my face grow hot. I hated Sasha for telling me what I had put out of my own mind a thousand times. "That's different," I said. "Things are never going to get better here."

"That's not true. I've seen your grandmother's poems printed, and we've had a real election. Everyone is saying that now that Yeltsin is in, the Communist party is done for. You surely know from your grandfather all about the changes Yeltsin is making. He's sweeping out the crooks."

"Yes, but the Communists are threatening to take over again, and then it would be just like it was."

"The people will never let them run the country again," Sasha said. "Why can't you see how things are improving?"

"We're not talking about me. It's you who will get into trouble."

"I can take care of myself, Tanya. Go home and think over what foolishness you are planning and leave me alone."

I hurried away without turning back to look in Sasha's direction. Everything I saw on the walk home irritated me. People looked tired and shabby, the children cross. The goods in the stores were either ugly or so expensive, no one but families like Vera's could afford them. Why shouldn't I try to better myself? Who was Sasha to preach to me? A little boy chasing a ball bumped into me, and I snarled, "Look where you are going." He gave me such a wounded look, I was ashamed. To cheer myself up, I wandered along the Fontanka River to the Anichkov Bridge, with its two pairs of bronze horses. I loved the horses, which always looked to me like the greatest ballet artists in the world, vaulting into the air with power and grace. Tsar Nicholas I gave the first horses away to a Prussian king who admired them. When they were replaced, Nicholas gave them away again, this time to the king of Naples. Once more they were replaced, and then during the Great Patriotic War they were buried to protect them during the bombing. It was awful to imagine the proud beasts imprisoned underground. "Like Russia," I thought, "a great country imprisoned by a corrupt government."

When a hard rain began to fall, I headed for home.

I had put Sasha and his troubles out of my mind, so I was unprepared to find him at my doorstep, his wet hair clinging to his head like a black helmet. "Sasha," I asked, "what's happened? You look like the world has come to an end."

He grabbed me by the shoulders. "Tanya, you have to help me. It's something terrible. You were right and I was wrong. It's the icon. Brompton has the real one."

"That's impossible. You wrapped it up yourself. I saw the package."

"While we were gone, Grandmother changed it for the real one."

"She would never have done that. Nothing she owned was more precious to her."

"Tanya, don't tell me something I know perfectly well. Of course I know what the icon means to her. That's why I'm so upset. She *did* do it. I met Brompton at a restaurant and gave him the icon, and he gave me the money, although less than he promised, but that makes no difference. I'll give him back the money, but I must have Grandmother's St. Vladimir."

"You haven't told me how he got the real one."

"Grandmother knew what I was doing all along. She knew that it was dishonest. While I was gone, she switched the icons. When I discovered what she had done, she said, 'Sasha, I would rather lose the precious icon than have you do something dishonorable.' Tanya, when I heard those words, I nearly died. You have to help me get it back. Your aunt must know where Mr. Brompton is."

"Aunt Marya was visiting at our apartment before I left. She may still be there."

We raced up the stairway, vaulting over a drunken body and stumbling on his bottle. When I threw open the door, we found Aunt Marya and Mother talking over cups of tea. They looked at us as if we had gone mad.

"Tanya, Sasha, what is it? You are soaking wet. What were you doing out in the rain? Has something happened to Nadya Petrovna?"

"No—yes," Sasha said. "It is worse than that. I have nearly killed her."

"Sasha," Aunt Marya said, "come and sit down and catch your breath, then tell us exactly what is wrong."

Sasha slumped down on a chair but refused the cup of tea Mama offered. The story came out in a great rush. "So I have to get to Brompton at once, before he takes off with Grandmother's St. Vladimir. She will die without it."

"Don't be melodramatic," Aunt Marya said. "You needn't exaggerate. The facts are bad enough. You have been a fool, Sasha, but I understand how much you wanted that medicine for your grandmother. Now, let's see what we can do. First of all, your Mr. Brompton is staying at the Hotel Europa."

That was the hotel where Mama worked. Quickly Mama said, "The receptionist is a friend. I'll go down and use the phone in the apartment lobby and see if

Mr. Brompton has checked out."

In a moment she was back, breathless from the climb. "It's a disgrace to have to live in an apartment building where men lie sprawled on the stairway."

"Mama, quickly, tell us what you found out."

"He is still there and has ordered a car to pick him up in an hour. He's in room three twenty-four. They are very strict about whom they let into the hotel. If you aren't a guest, you have to show some reason for being there. My friend said if anyone asked, to say you were there to pick up a package from Mr. Brompton. Look for her at the desk and she will pretend to ring Brompton, but she won't or he would never let you in. Her name is Nastya."

Sasha bolted toward the door and I was right behind him. "Where are you going, Tanya?" Mother called.

"With Sasha," I said. "I don't trust him to keep a cool head."

The hotel was only two blocks away. As I hurried

to keep up with Sasha, I asked, "How did you know Mr. Brompton had the real icon?"

"I didn't want him to have an image of Vladimir that was exactly like Grandmother's, so I put just a faint speck of blue on Vladimir's sleeve. No one would have noticed. When I got back from delivering the package with what I thought was the false icon, I looked up at the icon on the wall. There was the speck of blue! For a moment I thought St. Vladimir had made a miracle to punish me and then I saw Grandmother's face. There is no time to talk, Tanya—just hurry."

When we were within sight of the doorman, I made Sasha slow down. "If we look upset, they will be suspicious and never let us in."

As it was the doorman stopped us. When Sasha explained our errand, the doorman said, "It won't take two to pick up a package."

"Must I wait out here in the rain?" I said, giving the doorman my sweetest smile.

He grinned at me. "I'll put up an umbrella and you can keep me company."

"I would love to," I said, "but I don't think the hotel would approve."

"You are right there. Go ahead, but wait just inside the door."

Once inside the hotel I was intimidated by its splendor. A year before, as a special treat, Mama had taken me for tea in the hotel café. The café had a glass roof and even on that winter day was filled with flowering plants.

Sasha and I went at once to the reception desk, where Nastya was waiting for us. "Svetlana said there would be just the young man."

"I'm Svetlana's daughter," I assured her. "It's important that I talk with the man as well."

She looked doubtful. "You aren't going to make any trouble?"

We assured her that we would be only a moment and she nodded in the direction of the elevators.

Sasha knocked on the door of room 324.

"Who is it?" We recognized Brompton's voice.

We had decided a woman's voice would make Brompton less suspicious. "It's the concierge," I said. "I have some information about your car."

The door opened and an amazed and angry Brompton peered out at us. "Why are you here?" he demanded.

Sasha pushed past him and into the room. I followed, shutting the door behind me.

"What do you think you are doing? Get out at once. You have your money. Are you trying to hold me up?" Brompton reached for the phone.

Sasha threw a bundle of rubles onto the desk. "Here is the money—only hand back the icon."

"Nonsense. Of course I won't hand it back."

"It was a mistake," Sasha said. "I must have it."

"What Sasha means," I hastened to say, "is that his grandmother is very upset about selling the icon. You know how sick she is. She will die without it."

"That's superstitious nonsense," he said. "Now get out of here."

I stepped between them, afraid Sasha would throttle him. "Listen," I said in the most authoritative voice I could manage, "my grandfather is friends with lots of people in the new government. They are very strict about taking original art, and especially valuable icons, out of the country. If you don't give it back, my grandfather will report you to the customs officers at the airport. You'll end up in a Russian jail instead of on a plane."

Mr. Brompton was so angry, he could hardly speak. His face was red and puffed up. He turned to Sasha. "I don't understand. You wanted to sell it. What happened?"

"I told you," I said. "Sasha's grandmother is very upset." I walked toward the phone.

"No, wait." Mr. Brompton strode over to the suitcase on his bed and began pulling out shirts and underwear. When he got to the bottom of the suitcase, he gave us a wary look. With a shrug, he began to remove the lining of the suitcase, and underneath was the package with the icon. Sasha grabbed the icon and headed for the door.

"Wait," I said. I took the package from Sasha and unwrapped it while a furious Mr. Brompton looked on. I asked, "Is it the right one?"

Sasha, now close to tears, nodded.

As we left the hotel, the doorman winked at me. "Come by sometime when I'm about to go off duty."

We took the steps to Sasha's apartment two at a time. He knelt beside his grandmother. "Tanya and I got it back." He blurted out the story. "You don't hate me?" he asked.

"Sasha, Sasha," his grandmother said, stroking his hair. "What you were doing was breaking my heart, but what could I say? You were doing it for me. And God forgive me, I don't want to die and leave you. But even worse than death would be knowing that your love for me had made you do a dishonorable thing."

Sasha stood up, brushing the tears from his face. He plucked the icon he had painted from the wall and picked up a brush thick with black paint.

Before he could smear the black paint over the icon, his grandmother snatched it from his hand. "No, Sasha. It must hang beside the true St. Vladimir. You did what you did for love of me. Every time I look at your icon, I will think of that. It's as precious to me as my own St. Vladimir." She smiled. "And now with two such miraculous icons, I will surely improve."

CHAPTER 9

THE DANGEROUS ERRAND

At night Sasha's words: "Look what you plan to do—cheat the ballet that has trained you and made you the fine ballerina you are," kept me awake, but the next day Vera would be there to tug me in the other direction, talking of all the excitement of Paris. "Tanya, you are sure to be a great success. You will perform in theaters all over the world."

To tell the truth, there was little time for thinking of anything. There were new costumes for the tour, so in addition to practicing for hours we had to stand still for fittings. *The Firebird* had been completely revised, requiring additional work. In the August heat the rehearsal room was punishing. We had to wring out our practice leotards when we took them off. The Leningrad summer was rushing by, and I saw it only in snatches on my way from the theater to the apartment and back.

The week before we were to leave, Maxim Nikolayevich had a fight with the choreographer. Finally, in a temper, he sent everyone home for the afternoon. I went at once to Sasha's to beg him to come out with me. I was happy to see Nadya Petrovna was a little stronger.

"I was so relieved to have St. Vladimir back, I have been improving ever since. Don't tell me the icon has not performed a miracle. Yes, Tanya, take Sasha out with you. He spends all his time at his painting. The poor boy needs an airing."

"Grandmother, I am no goosefeather quilt to be taken out and shaken, but I can see Tanya needs a little airing herself."

The city was full of summer afternoon. The kiosks

were selling ice cream. Women were in summer dresses. Shops had set out pots of geraniums and petunias. We saw a few soldiers walk by, their caps pushed back on their heads, their collars open. In the Summer Garden where we settled on a patch of grass, the fountains were attracting children who dashed surreptitiously in and out of the flowing water while the attendant's back was turned.

Sasha lay down and closed his eyes. "Are you going to fall asleep and leave me sitting here?" I asked.

Sasha peered at me from beneath his long black lashes. "How can you talk, Tanya? Aren't you going to leave me, and not for a few minutes but forever?"

"Sasha, it's no good discussing it. Anyhow, if Yeltsin has his way, people will be able to travel in and out of the country. You can come and live in Paris."

"Visit Paris, yes. I long to see their museums, but live in Paris! Never. I'm a Russian. My art is Russian. Why would I leave this country just when it's finally going to be free?"

"Don't talk politics to me, Sasha. I hear it all the time at home. My family sit around the kitchen table and argue as if what they say can make a difference."

"It does make a difference. Your grandmother has been writing poems about freedom of the heart and mind for years, and without your grandfather risking his neck, Yeltsin wouldn't be where he is. Have you forgotten your past, Tanya? Your great-grandfather died from his days in a prison camp and your great-grandmother was exiled to Siberia. Your own grandparents were sent away after the war just because they had been heroes of Leningrad. You should be proud of them—you shouldn't be running away."

I jumped up and stood over Sasha, suppressing an urge to give him a kick. "I'm not running away. I'm going to live in a country were there is freedom."

Sasha was on his feet. "That's someone else's freedom. What about freedom in your own country?"

"I don't believe it will ever come."

"If you have so little faith, then you ought to leave."

We were standing there glaring at each other when Sasha put his arms around me and held me. I could smell all the old familiar smells of turpentine and varnish and something he used to tame his hair. I said, "I don't care about the country, but I hate leaving my family and leaving you."

"Don't leave. Stay and marry me."

I was startled into silence, but it took me only a moment to realize how impossible that would be. "How could we marry? You haven't finished school. We would have no place to live and no money." As soon as I dismissed the idea, I saw how much I liked it. If I stayed, in a few years Sasha would be out of school. Perhaps he would find a job teaching, or maybe his paintings would sell. I would be dancing more roles. What if I gave lessons as well? If, if, if. With the way things were now in Russia, it was an impossible dream.

We were holding hands and the fight had gone out of both of us. "Sasha, you'll be a famous artist and your paintings will be in the Paris galleries, so you will be traveling to Paris all the time."

"And you will be a world-famous ballerina and will come back to perform in your native Russia, where everyone will crowd around you and I will have to get in line to have a word with you."

We were laughing now and the arguing was behind us. But the words of the quarrel were still in our hearts, and when we said good-bye, the laughter disappeared altogether. I went away wondering if the dream I had chosen would make me as happy as the dream I was abandoning.

At the apartment it felt as if everyone in the family was holding their breath. It was clear that though no one seemed to know what it would be, something important was about to happen. Night after night I had found the family sitting around the kitchen table, discussing politics, more excited now than ever. Everyone had an opinion; voices were raised and fists pounded.

Grandfather complained, "Gorbachev is back at his dacha on the Black Sea, walking over marble floors and splashing around in his very own swimming pool. Meanwhile the starving miners are still on strike and industry is shutting down for lack of coal. All the money is going to the military."

"What is this treaty that is about to be signed?" Mama asked.

"It's Yeltsin's idea and Gorbachev has had to agree," Grandfather said. "Ukraine, Georgia, and all the other republics will have their own governments but will still be a part of the Soviet Union. I suppose it is like Australia's and Canada's relationship with the United Kingdom. The arrangement makes sense, but the old-line Communists are furious about giving the republics any independence."

"What is the difference then between Gorbachev and Yeltsin? Why is everyone taking sides?" Aunt Marya wanted to know.

"It's very simple," Grandfather said. "Gorbachev

is against private property, and Yeltsin is for it. Gorbachev tries to clean up the corruption in the Communist party, and Yeltsin says as long as we have a one-party system, we will never clean up the corruption. He says the Communist party has to go. The most important difference is that Yeltsin wants everyone to be able to vote."

"There is something else," Grandmother Yelena said. "Gorbachev has started to censor the newspapers and the magazines again. No one is taking my poems now, because my husband is fighting for Yeltsin."

"Gorbachev and Yeltsin can fight all they want to," Papa said. "The real danger is with the old Communist party members. They see their days are numbered. In a democratic country they won't be running things anymore."

"You are exactly right," Grandfather said. "Look for a last gasp, a last move on the part of the Communist party to take over the country."

I thought as usual Grandfather was just looking for a fight. After a few minutes of listening to the discussion I kissed everyone good night and pulled the curtains on my little cubbyhole. I didn't care about politics. I was going to be far away. For the thousandth time I took my suitcase from under my bed. My clothes for the trip had been packed and repacked. Tucked among the clothes were pictures of the family.

When I had asked for them, Mama had said, "Tanya, you are only going to be away for a little while. Surely you can remember us for so short a time."

"I've never been away from you, Mama. Let me have the pictures. I'll take good care of them." Reluctantly she took them from their frames and gave them to me.

The troupe was to leave for Moscow on August nineteenth. We would take the overnight train to Moscow, remain in the capital for two days, and then fly to Paris. We were all excited, for none of us had been on a plane and most of us had never been to Moscow or even on a train. Since I had been packed and ready to go for weeks, there was little preparation. The hard part was saying good-bye to those I loved. Mama must have sensed something in my behavior, for the morning before I was to leave, as we were sitting at the table having a second glass of tea, she put her hand on mine. "Tanya, is there something you aren't telling me?"

I could feel my cheeks burning. "What do you mean?"

"You seem so sad. I would have thought you would be thrilled at going on the tour."

"It's just that I've never been away from home before."

"You will be back before you know it. A couple of weeks is nothing when you have so much excitement ahead of you. You must write down everything so that you can tell us all about it. Now Papa and I have a surprise for you." Mama gave me a carefully wrapped package. Inside was a small camera. "There, you see. You'll take pictures of everything, and you'll be able to show us what you have seen when you get home."

All I could think of was putting pictures in an envelope and sending them back, and of what a rebuke that would be to Mama and Papa, who had sacrificed to buy me the camera.

Aunt Marya brought me a lovely silk scarf. "It belonged to a friend of mine and will bring you good luck," she said. "When you are in my beloved city of Paris, you must think of me."

Grandmother gave me a book of French poems. "They will help you understand the soul of the French," she promised.

Sasha came by for a final farewell. In front of the family we had to hide our two secrets: how much we cared for each other and our worry that we might never again see each other. When he left, he gave me a small parcel. "Open it when I'm gone. And keep it with you to protect you." Inside I found a miniature of St. Vladimir, so small it fit into the palm of my hand. Sasha had made a perfect copy of Nadya Petrovna's icon.

Grandfather's gift was the strangest gift of all, though it wasn't exactly a gift. It was the early afternoon of the day I was to leave, only an hour or so before I was to meet the others at the theater, where we would board a bus for the Moscow train station. I had already said good-bye to Mama and Papa, who had both left for work. Grandmother was at a writers' meeting. Grandfather and I were alone. He had been out and had just returned with a worried expression on his face. He began to pace back and forth in the tiny apartment. He was large and the apartment small, so the pacing took only a few steps each way. For the last two days Grandfather had acted strangely, all but looking over his shoulder as if he expected some calamity to appear. He had pored over the newspaper and spent long hours with his political friends, coming home late at night. He wore a worried frown all day long and was given to making gloomy predictions about the fate of the country.

Mama had asked, "Papa, why the worried look? Your Yeltsin is president of Russia and gaining in popularity every day."

Grandfather replied, "The stronger Yeltsin gets, the more the old guard in the Communist party plot to get rid of him and take the country back."

As I was strapping on my backpack, Grandfather stopped his pacing and said, "I must have a word with you, Tanya. There is a moment each spring just before I jump into the Neva River with its chunks of ice when I think, 'Georgi, you are a fool,' but I take the plunge. This is such a moment. I had not wanted to involve you in something dangerous, but I must. You would not be my granddaughter if you were unwilling to take a risk to save Russia."

"Me? Grandfather, what can you mean? What could I possibly do?" My heart skipped a beat, for I knew my grandfather could not always tell the difference between bravery and recklessness.

"Here in Leningrad phones are tapped and mail is censored. It is the same for the deputies in the parliament building in Moscow." Grandfather gave me a long look. "If you would agree to carry a letter, Tanya, to a certain deputy in Moscow, you will be doing your country a great service. We have come to the moment when Russia's fate will be decided. If you are reluctant to do it, you have only to tell me. I will surely understand."

I knew there was danger—that it might be the end of my dream of escaping Russia, that I might even be arrested—but Sasha's accusation that I was running away and betraying all that my grandparents and great-grandparents had suffered for our country still hurt. Here was an opportunity to prove him wrong. "I'll do it, Grandfather. But will they let me into the parliament building?"

"Russian tourists sightseeing in Moscow often go there to visit the deputy from their own town to lobby for some request or other. How suspicious could anyone be of a young ballerina making a dutiful pilgrimage to the seat of the government? Here is a letter of introduction to Lev Petrovich, one of the deputies from Leningrad. There is nothing suspicious in the letter. It says only that you have a petition from his Leningrad constituents begging him to apportion more money for the training of ballet dancers, a perfectly natural request coming from you. And here is the confidential letter for Lev Petrovich, which you must guard with your life. Lev Petrovich, like me, is a Yeltsin man, and this letter will let him know the names of those he can trust here in Leningrad in the event of a coup."

I could hardly believe what I was hearing. "A coup!"

"An alliance of the military and the old Communists, both of whom see their power slipping away, is going to try to take over the country. Gorbachev's days are numbered, and they know that when Yeltsin is in charge of the country, he means to get rid of the Communist party. If the alliance succeeds, we will be back to censorship and to people being dragged away from their homes in the middle of the night. When the coup comes about—and we don't know when that will be, but it will be sooner rather than later—Lev Petrovich must know whom he can count on in Leningrad to oppose it. This letter will tell him."

Grandfather handed me an envelope and I hastily put it into my backpack, where, flimsy as it was, it felt as heavy as a stone. I was terrified but I knew I could not let Grandfather down. "You can trust me," I promised.

He reached into his pocket and gave me a handful of rubles. "Buy yourself something pretty in Paris," he said. His bear hug and the look of relief on his face swept away my fears.

Grandfather offered to send me in a taxi to the Kirov theater, but it was a warm summer afternoon, and though I couldn't tell him, I wanted to see the city one last time. As I walked along, I thought it ironic that just as I was leaving, Leningrad had never looked lovelier. Across the street from our apartment was the great semicircle of Kazan Cathedral, with its ninety-six columns and its dome topped with a golden spire. When the light was at just this slant, the shadows of the columns lay in black stripes across the cathedral square. In the canal the water shimmered gold. For a moment I did not see how I could leave the city. I knew I should be thinking only of what was ahead of me, of my escape and of Paris, but instead, there were tears in my eyes. It seemed impossible that I might never see the Prospekt again or walk along the Moika canal. The sight of the great Kirov Theater building with its magnificent entrance made my heart stand still. I saw what I would be giving up. Only the excitement of what I was carrying and the danger of my assignment in Moscow kept me from weeping.

I hurried to the back entrance, where the bus that would take us to the train station was waiting. We were like little children about to be treated to a trip to the zoo, excited at what was ahead and nervous about going out into the big world. Vera and Vitaly gave me big hugs, and even Marina winked at me. The back-biting and competitiveness were gone. We were the lucky ones, and on us depended the reputation of the Kirov. In the excitement I forgot for a moment what I must do as soon as I reached Moscow. That is, I forgot until I noticed a strange man and woman standing beside our bus.

"Who are they?" I asked Vitaly.

"Secret police agents from the KGB," Vitaly said. "They always accompany groups when they leave Russia. Never mind them. We have nothing to hide."

Guiltily I exchanged looks with Vera, who appeared to be pale and subdued. "Tanya, don't look in the direction of those agents, but I'm worried they know something about me."

"What do you mean?" Surely they couldn't read

our minds and know we were planning to defect to France.

"Yeltsin has the government looking into my father's business."

I had long guessed that the Chikovs' money came from some enterprise. Now I remembered how Grandfather had said that Yeltsin was cleaning up graft and corruption. "Surely that won't affect you," I said.

Vera shrugged. "I'll tell you more later."

Madame, dressed in a new suit and, miracle of miracles, wearing nylon stockings and high heels, gathered us like chickens and shepherded us onto the bus. At the last moment Maxim Nikolayevich hurried out of his Volga and clambered on board, a new silk scarf twisted dramatically about his neck; he was wearing some sort of jaunty beret that was meant to look Parisian. The bus took us down the Prospekt; past our apartment building; past the Gostiny Dvor,

Leningrad's department store, where I had wandered a hundred times picking out things I longed for but for which I never had the money; past the monument of Catherine the Great; across the Anichkov Bridge with its great bronze horses; past the bookstores where Sasha and I had looked for bargains, and at last to the Moscow station.

At the station everything was chaos. A hundred trains roared in and out each day. People pushed us out of the way, while the KGB agents stood to one side watching and Madame and Maxim Nikolayevich ran about keeping us in line. At last we settled into our compartments, stacking our suitcases and backpacks on the overhead racks. To save money we were traveling second class, so there would be no bunks to sleep on. For dinner there was a snack bar with sandwiches and soda. The good news was that the KGB agents were traveling first class.

With the agents a safe two railway cars away, Vera took me aside. "The government has sent men into

Papa's office to examine his books. I know, Tanya, that Papa buys and sells where he shouldn't buy and sell, but still he is my papa and I'm worried. Just before we left, he gave me some jewelry to take to Paris. I'm to sell it. When I saw the KGB agents, I thought they were after me, but Madame said they always go on such trips.

"That is not the most important news," Vera went on, her voice now in a whisper. "Papa and Mama are making plans to escape to Paris as well. They know they won't be allowed to bring anything valuable with them—that's why they gave the jewelry to me."

All I could think of was how heartless the Chikovs were to put Vera in so risky a position. It was true that I, too, was taking a chance in carrying the letter for Grandfather, but that was in a noble cause; the Chikovs were endangering Vera only for money.

Vitaly called, "What are you two whispering about? You're missing all the sights." After that, to avoid suspicion Vera and I joined the others. For most of us in the troupe it was our first trip out of Leningrad. The August evening was hot, and we opened the windows and leaned out to see the scenery, getting cinders in our eyes and letting soot into the compartment. It was a wonder to have the country fly by, but by midnight the novelty of the trip had worn off and the compartment quieted. We curled up on the seats, resting our heads on our backpacks. Vitaly and Vera were sound asleep, but I shifted restlessly, thinking of the envelope that lay beneath my head, and of what would happen if it were discovered.

CHAPTER 10

TANKS IN THE STREET

At eight in the morning, yawning and stretching, we hurried off of the train and onto the bus that would take us to our Moscow hotel. We pushed against one another to get next to a window and view the city we had heard so much about. Moscow was larger and busier than Leningrad, with wide streets crowded with automobiles. Madame pointed out the Bolshoi Theater, and we all agreed it was not as handsome as the Kirov. Suddenly the Kremlin was in front of our eyes. How we stared. The Kremlin had started out as an ancient fortress whose towered brick walls still stood. Behind the walls were the buildings we knew from our school days, when every child learned about the Kremlin. We saw Assumption Cathedral with its brightly colored domes and the bell tower of Ivan the Great. Inside Red Square was the Lenin mausoleum where Lenin lay preserved in his glass coffin like some exotic tidbit in a jar.

In front of the Kremlin I could see a part of Red Square with the cathedral of St. Basil the Blessed and another great cathedral that had been turned into the State History Museum. Just ahead of us was the platform where each year, on the anniversary of the revolution, Stalin had stood to review miles of soldiers and weapons. Vitaly asked, "Tanya, what's wrong? You look a little green."

"I'm just carsick," I said. "First the train and then the bus." I wasn't carsick at all. I was frightened of what I had agreed to do. Though Stalin had been dead for nearly forty years, just the thought of how he had sent millions to their deaths for opposing him both frightened me and made me more sure than ever that

I must carry out my promise to Grandfather. But the city was so large. How would I get from our hotel to the parliament building? The task seemed impossible.

The bus was traveling along the Moscow River and passing a large green space. "Gorky Park," Madame said. "And here on Novy Arbat Street is our hotel. The tall building over there is the trade center, and just beyond it that huge white building is the parliament, where Yeltsin and our deputies are at work. Now everyone off the bus, and don't forget to look around to be sure you have all your things."

The parliament building was right there in front of me! I had no excuse now for not delivering the letter. I hugged my backpack to me and followed the others off the bus. The first chance I had, I would slip out of my room and head for the parliament. The sooner I got it over with, the sooner I could breathe again.

As we crowded into the lobby of the hotel, I felt someone fling herself at me and give me a crushing hug. "Natalia!" I cried.

"Tanya, as soon as I knew you would be staying here, I camped out in the lobby. I've been waiting for hours to be sure I would be here to greet you. Oh, Tanya, I am so happy. I'm in the Moscow Choreography School. The ballet mistress says I am doing well, and one day I will be sure to dance with the Bolshoi. I go everywhere in Moscow. I know a little café in the Arbat where we can have breakfast."

"Natalia, give me a chance to catch my breath. I have been up all night. I couldn't sleep in the train. I'll just catch a few winks and meet you for lunch. We don't have anything scheduled until the performance of the Bolshoi tonight." There was nothing I wanted more than to hear of Natalia's adventures with the Bolshoi, but I had made Grandfather a promise, and I meant to keep it.

Natalia looked like a wounded puppy. "Listen," I said, "here is a special letter Uncle Fyodor has sent to you, and at lunch I'll give you all the news of the shelter." Reluctantly Natalia let me go, and I followed

Vera up to the hotel room I was to share with her. I thought having a whole room just to ourselves was a miracle, but Vera complained that there was no television set and no phone. "The soap in the bathroom is cheap. Why don't they put us up in a decent place?"

"Vera, you are spoiled. It seems like heaven to me." Never had I had a bathroom all to myself. I thought of soaking in a lovely bath with no one pounding on the door for a turn, but I settled for splashing some water on my face. "I have to run out for a few minutes. I'll be right back."

"I'll come with you. There's no reason to stay in this dreary place."

"I just want a few minutes by myself, Vera. I'll be right back. Anyhow, wouldn't it be better for you to stay here with your jewelry, where it's safe? You don't want to take any chances."

I ignored Vera's puzzled look and hurried out of the room. In the lobby I saw the two KGB agents loitering by the door. As I walked past them, the woman said, "You seem eager to go out."

"I forgot my lipstick," I said.

"You couldn't borrow some?" the man asked.

I gave him a withering look. "It wouldn't be the right shade." He shrugged as if I were too frivolous to bother with.

Once outside on the street with all the rushing cars and with people pushing rudely by me, I lost heart. I was ready to turn back when I noticed a large number of police on the streets. Rounding a corner, I saw a tank lumbering right down the center of the street as if it were a trolley car. Something was happening. I hurried along. The great white parliament building loomed over me. I made myself walk past the security guards as if I belonged there. At the desk I asked to see Lev Petrovich, showing the woman the official letter Grandfather had given me with the petition to ask for more money for our Leningrad ballet.

The woman behind the desk glanced at the petition and said, "The deputy is too busy to see you on such a small matter. I'll see that the petition is passed along."

"Please, just let the deputy know who I am. I am sure he is expecting me and has a photographer all ready to take a picture for the Leningrad newspaper. He will be very angry if you send me away."

The woman gave me a suspicious look. "If he bites off my head for bothering him, it will be your fault."

She dialed a number and read out my name. With a disappointed look she indicated the bank of elevators. "It seems he will see you," she said. "Tenth floor."

When I reached the tenth floor, a tall, thin man with glasses resting on the end of his nose was waiting at the elevator to greet me. He ushered me by some secretaries and pulled me into his office. "I had a phone call from Georgi Mikhailovich telling me that his granddaughter was visiting Moscow and would stop by to request money for something or other. I knew he couldn't speak freely over the phone and guessed that you would have something of importance for me."

The man looked so intently at me, I was sure he could see into my backpack. I quickly handed him the letter, which he read at a gulp, nodding and repeating yes, yes as he went along. He must have been encouraged by what he read, for when he was finished, he smiled at me and said, "You were brave to bring this, Tanya."

"Lev Petrovich," I said, "I saw a tank on the street just a minute ago."

"I believe the coup is under way. We guessed it would come while Gorbachev was out of town, but we had no idea it would come so soon." He let out a sigh, so deep it must have traveled all the way up from his toes. "It may be that you have arrived in Moscow on the very day Russia loses her chance for freedom."

There were shouts. One of the secretaries called, "Lev Petrovich, come and look!"

We hurried to the window. There, crawling along on the street looking like a parade of giant beetles, were scores of tanks. Just behind them was a long line of trucks loaded with soldiers.

Someone switched on a radio. A man with the voice of an angry schoolmaster announced that Soviet President Mikhail Gorbachev, on vacation in the Crimea, had been replaced because of ill health. Power was being transferred to the vice president and to something called the Committee for a State of Emergency.

Lev Petrovich said, "That committee will be made up of the army and the KGB and the Communist party. They probably have Gorbachev under arrest. Now our only hope is the president of Russia, Boris Yeltsin, if he hasn't been arrested as well."

We could see hundreds of people pouring out of houses and buildings. They were gathering around the parliament building, shouting and shaking their fists at the tanks. The soldiers' guns at the ready kept the people from getting too close.

A moment later there was a great roar and the sound of breaking glass. The tanks were firing on the parliament! We dropped to the floor. After a moment everything was silent. When no more shots were fired, we slowly got up, everyone looking embarrassed at having been frightened. We brushed ourselves off and went back to the windows to see what our fate would be.

"If we are ever to have democracy in this country," Lev Petrovich said, "it must come from this building and on this day." For a moment he forgot the drama outside the building and turned to me. "I am sure you had no idea you would find yourself in the middle of a battle, but I have no doubt that any grandchild of Georgi Mikhailovich will know how to be brave."

There was a shout from the hallway. "Yeltsin is here!" We crowded into the hallway, and there hurtling toward us, two stairs at a time, was a giant of a man, his hair uncombed, his shirt half out, and wearing under his jacket a heavy military-looking vest that I guessed at once must be bulletproof. "They lied to the soldiers," he cried, "telling them they were being sent into Moscow to round up draft dodgers. Even so, some of the soldiers may go along with the coup, but there will be soldiers who will come over to our side. I am sure of it."

Someone called, "The television and radio stations have been taken over."

"We will have to find another way to get the truth out," Yeltsin said. "We have to tell them that Gorbachev is under arrest in his dacha in the Crimea, but that the president of Russia, me, Boris Yeltsin, is right here on duty in the parliament. I and all the deputies will fight to the death to preserve Russia's new freedom. Everyone in the city must come out and support us.

"Lev Petrovich, get your people together and print a leaflet—print thousands of them." Yeltsin began to dictate the words for the leaflet:

Storm clouds of terror and dictatorship are gathering over the whole country. The enemy must not be allowed to bring eternal night. Citizens of Russia, I believe in this tragic hour you can make the right choice. The honor and glory of Russian men of arms shall not be stained with the blood of the people.

Before I knew it, I was gathering the leaflets as they came from the printing machine. I ran down the stairway to the entrance, where people were grabbing the leaflets to post all over the city. When soldiers stopped us, we carried the leaflets to all the offices and flung them out the windows to the people who waited below.

The streets were a solid sea of people, thousands and thousands of people. Some were approaching the tanks and arguing with the soldiers. Some were putting flowers in the gun barrels. Yeltsin wanted to talk with the people, but even though he had his bulletproof vest, everyone was afraid of snipers. "They would like nothing better than a chance to shoot you down, Boris Nikolayevich," Lev Petrovich warned Yeltsin.

Down below us a microphone had been hastily put up. One after another, speakers stood up and addressed the crowd, urging them to oppose the coup. Surprisingly, the soldiers and the tanks did nothing to stop them.

"Look!" someone cried. "There is Rostropovich!" The most famous cellist in the world, a man who had been exiled from the Soviet Union but who had come back from America for a visit, was standing there waving a Kalashnikov rifle. "I love you," he shouted to the crowd. "I am proud of you." The soldiers didn't dare shoot at the man who was famous all over the world.

After seeing Mikhail Rostropovich, nothing could hold Yeltsin back. Yeltsin said, "I'm going out there." He combed his unruly hair, put his necktie back on, and strode out the front door. We hung out of the windows, holding our breath. He was a large and easy target. One bullet and there would be no one to rally around, no one to lead the country into real freedom. The soldiers were standing up in their tanks watching Yeltsin approach. The crowd was shouting and cheering. I stopped breathing.

Yeltsin paused in front of a tank. Suddenly he was climbing up the side of the tank, his big awkward body supported and pushed by a churning crowd. The soldier in the tank not only did not stop him, but amazingly even gave him a hand up. Yeltsin was astride the tank and waving to the crowd. People swarmed around the tank. "Citizens of Russia," he shouted above the roar. He urged the soldiers not to take part in the coup, and he appealed to the whole country to support democracy. From everywhere came the shout of "Yeltsin, Yeltsin." He climbed down and came inside, his hair tousled, sweat running down his face.

As we watched from the window, we were amazed to see that some of the gunners on the tanks were turning the barrels of their guns away from the parliament building. A great cheer went up, and we all hugged one another.

We printed leaflets all afternoon without stopping. It was only when someone mentioned that we had not had anything to eat that I realized I was starving. A deputy named Nemtsov had an idea. "The American embassy is close by. I'll give them a call and tell them we have no food. Surely they will understand that we are fighting for democracy in here."

Within an hour a van drove up with the name of the United States on it. There was some discussion between the soldiers and the driver, but at last the driver and his helper got permission to bring the food into the parliament. We sat around, the men in shirt-sleeves, the women with their shoes kicked off, gobbling down sandwiches and watching the television. All the news had been cut off. Incredibly, Moscow TV was showing a movie of the Bolshoi Ballet dancing *Swan Lake*. For a moment I forgot where I was and sat there intent on the performance of the prima ballerina. The others were all talking about the coup in worried tones. Finally Lev Petrovich asked, "Tanya, at what are you staring?"

Without thinking, I said, "At her *brisé volé en avant*. The way she slides her foot after the *demi-plié* is very awkward."

There was complete silence, and then everyone began to laugh. "Well, as long as there is nothing more to worry about than a *demi-plié*," Lev Petrovich said, "there is hope for Russia's future."

As night came on, thousands stayed to cheer Yeltsin and to demand that the tanks leave, but the tanks remained. Reporters from all over had crowded into the building and were sending out reports of the coup around the world. The fax machines rattled away and the phones kept ringing. We heard a loud cheer go up from the crowd as they learned there was a huge rally against the coup in Leningrad's Palace Square. I was sure Grandfather would be leading it.

Moments later the joy turned to shock. Three men had been killed. One of the men had thrown a canvas over the window of a tank to blind the driver so the tank could not move. Once the tank stopped, the man jumped up trying to get inside. He was shot by a soldier and died instantly. When his two friends tried to pull his body away from the advancing tank, they were shot. After that Lev Petrovich and several other deputies patrolled the hallways with rifles at the ready. They were obviously unused to guns, and their awkwardness with them made us feel more uneasy than safe. Even the great Rostropovich was guarding Yeltsin's office with his Kalashnikov rifle.

Outside, the tanks were quiet and the crowd settled in for the night. The continual sound of their portable radios was like waves of a sea washing in. It was nearly light when I finally put my head down on a desk and closed my eyes, thinking what a story I would have to tell Grandfather, forgetting that when the coup was over, however it turned out, I would be far away in Paris.

In the morning I headed for the bathroom with the other women to splash water on my face. We shared combs and lipsticks, trying to put ourselves in some kind of order. The men slicked down their hair with water, but they all had a day's growth of beard. In spite of a rain that had begun to fall, the crowd had spent the night in the streets. "There must be a hundred thousand people out there," Lev Petrovich said.

All night famous people had come to entertain the crowd and encourage opposition to the coup. The comic Gennady Khazanov gave a funny imitation of Gorbachev. The poet Yevgeni Yevtushenko, who was a friend of my grandmother's, read a poem to the crowd. I remembered how he had once written that we all needed to be tormented by our consciences. As long as we hear within ourselves the cry, "What have *I* done," he wrote, "then something can be done with this world." On this day tormented consciences were winning, but what of mine? What would my conscience say to me for running away from Russia?

Yeltsin walked out onto a balcony. When he appeared, a tremendous shout went up. Lev Petrovich pushed his way onto the balcony with the other deputies, pulling me with him. "There will be cameras out there, Tanya. Now is your chance to be famous. These pictures will be in newspapers all around the world. Think how proud your grandfather will be to see you here."

"Democracy will win out," Yeltsin shouted. He promised to stay in the parliament building for as long as it took for the leaders of the coup to be brought to justice. A wild cheer went up.

By noon of the second day we were all hungry again. The food from the American embassy had long since been eaten. As we looked out the window, we saw a man make a dash for the parliament building. He was carrying a load of boxes. Behind him came another man also with a tower of boxes. Pizzas! More pizzas came, and we sat around the desks drinking soda from the machines and eating the pizzas, tomato and cheese all over our faces.

Just as we finished our feast, startling news swept the parliament: In front of the KGB building the people had pulled down the statue of the founder of the secret police. Someone called to say Gorbachev had been released and the leaders of the coup had ordered the troops out of the city. The great armored beasts began to move away from the parliament. A rumor spread that Gorbachev was furious over his arrest by the KGB and would issue a decree to put an end to the Communist party.

I had lost all track of time, but now I realized that unless I left at once, I would miss the flight to Paris. Lev Petrovich shook my hand. "They will be cheering in St. Petersburg, and your grandfather will be leading them," he said to me. For a moment I didn't take in his words. Then for the first time I realized what had happened. "St. Petersburg," he had said. Because of the coup's defeat, my city had its rightful name back. Leningrad was once more St. Petersburg. I said the city's real name over and over. Leningrad was gone forever. I had watched it happen. I had been a part of it. I could see that change was possible, and my heart filled with hope. How could I leave Russia?

CHAPTER 11

PARIS

I was just in time to hug Natalia, promise to write to her, and board the bus to the airport. On the bus I had to tell my story over and over. Even Madame and Maxim Nikolayevich hung upon my words, but at the end of my story Madame said, "I hope you did not forget your practice sessions while you were in the parliament building. Did you have your toe shoes with you?"

I had to confess that I did not.

We all tried to pretend that soaring thousands of feet into the air and flying along at hundreds of miles an hour was nothing to us. Vera and I held hands at the takeoff and landing, and I was glad Sasha's St. Vladimir was traveling with us. I wondered how the promise of a new Russia could change things for Sasha and me. I only knew I couldn't wait to see Sasha and tell him my story. Staying in Paris seemed less exciting than returning to the new Russia, but how was I to tell that to Vera?

Madame announced that on the way to our hotel the bus driver would swing by a few of the best-known Paris landmarks. "Take a good look, for after this you will see nothing of the city but the route to and from the opera house, where you will be practicing from dawn to dusk."

Our first glimpse of Paris was through dirty bus windows. There was the Eiffel Tower and Notre Dame Cathedral and the river Seine. I could feel how ancient the city was, hundreds of years older than St. Petersburg. Handsome as the buildings were, most were of gray stone. The buildings appeared drab when I compared them with the pinks and greens and blues

of St. Petersburg's buildings. On that August afternoon the green trees along the wide boulevards made
everything lively, but I imagined how cheerless it
would be in the winter if I stayed on. There would be
nothing but bare branches and somber stone buildings
to keep me company, and at the end of the day no
familiar and loving faces to greet me.

While I was searching for a way to let Vera know
that I wanted to return to Russia, Vera exclaimed over
everything, seeing it as her new home. She had no
reservations about the city. "Tanya, look at all the
shops and stores. I'm going to go into every one of
them."

Madame put an end to Vera's ambition. The
moment we were unpacked, we were bused to the
Paris Opéra. Even Madame was a little intimidated by
the size of the opera house. The ornate building rose
high up into the air and was crowned by a great dome,
upon which stood a golden statue of Apollo, the god
of music and poetry. It must have covered several acres

and was approached by a wide stairway, on which lovers sat in the summer sunshine absorbed in one another. I lagged behind, thinking of Sasha, but Vera grabbed my arm and pulled me up the steps. Right outside the entrance for everyone to see were posters advertising the Kirov Ballet.

I think Madame was gratified to find the rehearsal rooms were as cramped and unadorned as our own. In no time we had changed into our leotards and toe shoes, and between the demands of Madame and Maxim Nikolayevich we practiced until our shoes wore out and our bodies were one intense ache. Then we practiced some more.

A dinner had been arranged for us in the hotel dining room, and we fell upon it like lions and tigers, reveling in the tasty soup and chicken stew and the luxurious plates of fresh fruit and cheese. Because our first performance was the following evening, rehearsals were called for early the next morning. Most of the exhausted troupe were satisfied to fall into bed, but Vera begged me to take a walk with her. "There's something I must do and I want company." I was tired and longed for bed, but I agreed, knowing I would soon have to tell Vera I was going to desert her.

Vera insisted we slip out the rear entrance of the hotel to avoid any questions by the KGB agents. She had a scrap of paper and a city map. Consulting an address written down on the paper, she led me up one street and down another; we strayed farther and farther from the hotel into a neighborhood of small shops and rough-looking cafés where I was conscious of men staring rudely at us. "Vera, we are going to be lost. Where are you taking me?"

"It should be just around the corner." She glanced at the slip of paper once more and then led me to the entrance of a shop with iron bars across the windows. The shop was closed, but she knocked on the door. A woman in a long black skirt and a soiled sweater reluctantly allowed us to come inside. "I want to talk with Monsieur Lepage." I saw Vera hand one of her father's business cards to the woman. The woman looked us up and down and then disappeared. Moments later an elderly man shuffled out and gave Vera a knowing smile. "*Bonsoir, bonsoir, mesdemoiselles*. What can I do for Monsieur Chikov's daughter?"

Vera reached into the pocket of her skirt and pulled out a handkerchief. Inside the handkerchief was a bracelet, bright gold with red and green stones. "How much for this?" Vera asked. The man appeared delighted with the bracelet. He mentioned a figure that I was sure I misheard. Vera shook her head. "That is too little. Papa says it is worth twice that amount." Then commenced an intense argument between Monsieur Lepage and Vera. At last the man handed Vera a stack of francs, which Vera stuffed into a large purse she was carrying.

The moment we were out of the shop, I said, "Vera, those were rubies and emeralds. Wherever did your father get it?"

"Papa puts all his money into gold and stones. It's a kind of insurance. You never know what the ruble will be worth from day to day."

I was horrified. "Vera, it's strictly against the law to carry something like that out of Russia, and how did your father get so much money he could buy a bracelet like that?"

"Tanya, don't be naive. You have guessed Papa deals on the black market. More and more countries are anxious for weapons, and Papa, as a former military officer, knows how to get hold of the arms the Russian army has abandoned. When he and Mama come over, they will be sure to be searched, so he sent the bracelet with me, just a poor ballerina whom no one would suspect. Papa said I could have a few of the francs for my own. I'll treat you to some perfume tomorrow."

Mikhail Grigoryevich Chikov was an evil man. He was buying weapons from dishonest men in the army who wanted to make money by selling the weapons to outlaw nations and terrorists, who could turn them on innocent people. I couldn't blame Vera for what her father did, or for the way her father was using her, but I resolved I would take no money from Vera for French perfume or anything else.

It looked as though the dishonest people were abandoning Russia, and it was not only Vera's family. Marina was my enemy once again, this time because I had taken Yeltsin's side. She had learned that her father was one of the men in the government who had organized the coup. Like Vera's family, Marina's family would have to leave Russia. If I ran away from Russia, I would be in bad company. I would be going in the wrong direction. More than ever, I knew I was right to plan to return home.

All the next day our excitement built up. We were nervous and irritable at rehearsal. Madame criticized and Maxim Nikolayevich shouted and even cried real tears, telling us that we would disgrace the Kirov forever with our awkwardness. Though I knew we were dancing better than we ever had, when I saw the immense stage, a stage large enough for four hundred performers, I was shaken. Looking out at tier upon tier of golden boxes, imagining two thousand people sitting there watching us, I did not see how I would get through the night.

Everything was new and different. We had to accustom ourselves to the opera house orchestra and they to us. While the Russian method of ballet has much of the French method, still there are differences. The French director of dance had problems with our choreography. The scenery had been designed for the Kirov Theater and was lost on the huge stage of the Paris Opéra. The costumes had been made especially for the tour, and we were wearing them for the first time. The strain of the trip and the increased practices had made many of us lose weight, and the wardrobe mistress's needle was flying to take in seams. No one believed we could put together a decent performance that evening.

Much to Marina's disgust, I was dancing Juliet, leaving her with a secondary role. I stood in the wings waiting to go on. At the first notes of the overture a wave of nausea swept over me, and I thought I would be sick. Vitaly must have seen me turn pale, for he grabbed my arm and pinched me. The next minute I was following the dancers onto the stage. I remember nothing after that until the coda, when all the principal dancers made their final appearance. A rolling thunder of applause came from the audience. There was a standing ovation. Ushers hurried onto the stage with bouquets. I found my arms full of roses. Backstage we hugged and kissed one another. There was a party in Maxim Nikolayevich's hotel room for the entire corps. I was too tired to go, but Vera went and returned after midnight to shake me awake and feed me caviar and chocolates.

The next day we crowded together in the breakfast room of the hotel to read the newspaper reviews of the ballet. Though the critics sang our praises, we heard nothing but harsh criticism from Madame and Maxim Nikolayevich. "Vitaly, your *grand jeté* looked like the cow jumping over the moon. Tanya, your extension was too brief. You must keep your leg high. Marina, your *entrechats* had all the grace of an egg-beater." Of course we all knew that Madame and Maxim Nikolayevich's criticism was to keep us from believing we could relax because the reviews were good, for we caught them poring over the reviews themselves, broad smiles on their faces.

Between the morning and afternoon rehearsals we were awarded a whole hour to see the city. "Hurry, Tanya," Vera said. I guessed she was headed to the Galeries Lafayette to spend some of her francs. I was about to send her on her way and head for the Louvre to buy postcards of the paintings for Sasha.

"No," Vera said. "You must come with me. They want us."

"Want us? Who wants us?"

"You fool. What have we been talking of all year?

There is a representative of the Paris Opéra who saw the performance last night. He came backstage, and I whispered a word to him about our wanting to defect and stay in Paris."

I should have told Vera long since that I was going back to Russia, but I was too cowardly. "Maybe you ought to talk with him and let me know what he says."

"Are you mad? You are the better dancer. He's sure to want you, but if he knows he can have you, he will take me as well." She looked at me. "You aren't getting cold feet?"

"Vera, it just doesn't seem fair to be thinking of deserting the Kirov when we have done so well as a troupe. Besides, after what has just happened, everything will change in Russia. We're going to be a democracy. In a few years we'll be like Paris, so there is no need to leave now."

"Leningrad like Paris! Not in our lifetime. I can't wait, Tanya. Even if I wanted to go back, with my parents coming here, there would be nothing for me to go back for. As a member of my family I might even be punished." Her face hardened. "Do what you like, Tanya, but at least come with me and help me get a place in the ballet here."

I trailed after her to the small café where the man had said he would meet with us. Every so often Vera made me stop, just as they did in mystery films, to study the reflections in the shop windows to be sure we weren't being followed. We sneaked into the café and joined a man whom Vera recognized, and who introduced himself as Monsieur Durant. He was gray-haired with a creased face, but I could tell he still had the muscular strength of a dancer. When the man saw us looking over our shoulders, he said, "You needn't worry. Those KGB agents are spending all their time on the telephone calling back to Moscow to see if they still have their jobs. The KGB won't have the power it had under the Communists."

He ordered coffee in thick white cups and croissants served with great lumps of butter and a whole pot of beautiful currant jam. That was what Paris would be like, I thought—every day something delicious—and I felt myself wavering.

He complimented us at once on the performance. "Extraordinary. One does not often see such a combination of fire and grace. Of course we have our own ballet at the opera house, so we are used to magnificent performances, for we see them every week."

Certainly there was nothing modest about the man, and I began to take a dislike to him, but Vera hung on his every word.

"We are always looking for new talent," he said, "and even from my limited observation of only one performance, I could see both of you are skilled dancers. Naturally every ballet company, no matter how excellent, will look for new talent to freshen the repertoire." He looked at us as if we were objects in a shop window.

Vera asked, "Then you would offer us positions if we stayed on after our troupe left?"

Monsieur Durant threw his hands out as if to say "of course."

Before I could stop myself, I said, "You would be very lucky to get Vera, but I'm going back to Russia."

The man frowned. "I understood you were both interested in remaining in Paris. To be perfectly frank with you, it was this young lady"—he nodded at me—"whom we were especially interested in. We have our own candidates for the *corps de ballet*."

Vera's face collapsed. I was afraid she was going to cry. I knew how much remaining in Paris meant to her. I thought of all the months she and I had dreamed of a future away from Russia, and now I was making it impossible for her. Her parents were deserting Russia. She had no one to return to there. With all my heart I wanted to go back to St. Petersburg, but how could I desert her when she needed me most? "Can you just give me until tomorrow to consider your offer?" Maybe I would think of a way for Vera to stay without me.

The man shrugged. "Yes, yes, of course. In the meantime I'll put together a proper contract, and we will meet here tomorrow at the same time."

On the way back to the hotel, Vera listed all the reasons for me to stay. "You would never be sorry," she said. But I knew I would be sorry—more than sorry, I would be miserable if I stayed in Paris.

Marina danced Juliet in the second performance, so in a secondary role I felt less pressure and was able to look about me at the tier upon tier of the opera house and at all those unknown faces watching us dance. There was an excitement in the audience that made me want to respond, made me want to be better than I had ever been. As we took our bows at the performance's end, I heard loud shouts of "Vera! Vera!" from the front row. There, waving wildly and blowing kisses toward the stage, were Mr. and Mrs. Chikov. They appeared backstage hugging Vera, filling her arms with flowers, and then carrying her off. As they left, they greeted me, but their greeting was cold. They knew it was Grandfather's man, Boris Yeltsin, who was closing down the black markets and chasing them out of Russia.

When Vera returned to our room in the hotel that evening, she said, "Tanya, I have wonderful news for you. I know you want to go back to Russia. Now if you want to return, you can. I'm not staying in Paris."

"Vera! I'm so happy you're coming back."

"No, don't misunderstand me, Tanya. I wouldn't think of going back to Russia, even if I could. My parents are going to South America. Papa is going to work with some men down there. They've promised him a lot of money because of his connections with the Russian army. It's useless for me to stay here. You heard the man this afternoon. He wanted you and not me. I'll never be a great dancer. With my parents far away, if I stayed here, I'd end up sharing a room with some other dancers from the ballet, and when I grew old, who would take care of me? Dancing isn't my life like it's yours. It was just a way to get out of Russia.

Papa says we will live like kings in South America."

All this was too much for me. I didn't have to oblige Vera by staying in Paris. I could go home with a clear conscience. But what about Vera? How could I let her go on to South America, where her father would be selling Russian arms to whoever could pay for them?

The day the tour ended, I pleaded with her. "Vera, listen to me. Don't go with your father. You have years ahead of you to be a fine dancer. I know you can do well. Don't give it up, and especially don't be a part of what your father is doing. Come back to St. Petersburg with me. You can live with us, and I promise my grandfather will protect you."

For a moment Vera was silent, and I hoped she had changed her mind, but she only said, "Tanya, you are a romantic. You think now everything will be perfect in Russia. Let me tell you there are still plenty of men left in Russia ready to buy and sell the country. Don't think for a minute that the KGB will just give up their power and welcome democracy. How long will it be before one of them comes to power and the repression starts all over again? And Tanya, what will you have when you go back to Russia? You'll have the same old dowdy clothes to wear and the same old beet soup for dinner. I'm not proud of what Papa does, but he's still my father and lots of people do what he is doing. If people mean to buy arms, why shouldn't he be the one to sell them? Why shouldn't I go with him and enjoy my life?" She put her arms around me and kissed me. A minute later I watched as she carried her small suitcase down the hall of the hotel.

It seemed like years since we had begun to dream of living in Paris. How could we have guessed that our world would change and we would change with it? I was sorry for Vera. I believed she was a good person, generous and brave, but she would have to tell herself lies to live with what her father did. Someday she would wake up and see how evil it was. By then it might be too late for her.

Vera said democracy would be impossible in Russia. Why should that be? All those years ago, when I was a child and dreamed of being a ballerina, I had thought only of how elegant I would look in my tutu and toe slippers, how I would dance across the stage, hardly touching the floor, how people would applaud my performance. What if I had known that ahead of me lay hours of exercises, aching limbs, tortured toes, Madame's cries of "You are hopeless," and everything else in my life—even Sasha whom I loved—pushed aside? I had started on the path, and no hour or day had been so difficult that I could not get through it, but taken all together, I don't know how I did it. Why shouldn't it be the same for Russia? Difficulties, troubles, and failures, and always the threat of corrupt leaders who would long for power, but after two thousand years, Russia had set out on a path to democracy. Even if there were bad times, why shouldn't it succeed? How could I not be there to see it happening?

Before our return to St. Petersburg, we were all

taken as a reward to the Eiffel Tower. Up we went in the elevator, except for Vitaly, who took the 1,652 steps two at a time. Below us were the treetops of Paris. We were so high that when I looked north and east, I almost thought I could see St. Petersburg in the distance, the city of Peter the Great, let down from the sky, new and shining.

GLOSSARY

Russian words

besprizorniki: neglected ones

devochka: a young girl

kefir: sour yogurt drink

pelmeny: dumplings filled with cabbage, meat, or cheese

perestroika: a new beginning, new thought

pirozhkovye: restaurant that sells *pelmeny*

pyshechnayas: doughnut shop

French ballet terms

arabesque: a pose in which a dancer stands on one leg with one arm extended in front and the other arm and leg extended behind

arqué: bowlegged

barre: a wooden bar attached horizontally to the wall of a rehearsal room and used by dancers for support

battement: a beating movement of the leg

brisé volé en avant: a beating movement that is broken off

chassé: a gliding movement

corps de ballet: all the dancers in a ballet troupe apart from the principal dancers

échappé: a movement from a closed position to an open one

en pointe: dancing on one's toes

enlèvement: lifting of a ballerina into the air by a male dancer

entrechat: a step in which the dancer jumps into the air and crosses her legs in front and then behind

extension: the extension of a raised leg

fouetté: a whipping around, either in a rapid turn or with one foot rapidly whipping in front and then in back of the other foot

jarreté: knock-kneed

jeté: a leap with the legs extended

pas de deux: a dance done by two people

pirouette: a spin

plié: a bending of the knees with the back held straight

relevé: a rising on the toes

sur les pointes: up on one's toes

tour en l'air: a turn in the air

AUTHOR'S NOTE

Russians refer to World War II as the Great Patriotic War.

While the Kirov Ballet of St. Petersburg is very real, and one of the great ballet companies of the world—some would say the greatest—their tour to Paris in August 1991 was all of my own imagining.

My descriptions of the coup and many of the events that took place at the parliament building in August 1991 are based on actual happenings.